1991

1991

HOW P. V. NARASIMHA RAO MADE HISTORY

SANJAYA BARU

ALEPH

ALEPH

ALEPH BOOK COMPANY
An independent publishing firm
promoted by *Rupa Publications India*

First published in India in 2016
by Aleph Book Company
7/16 Ansari Road, Daryaganj
New Delhi 110 002

ISBN: 978-93-84067-68-7

1 3 5 7 9 10 8 6 4 2

Printed and bound in India by Replika Press Pvt. Ltd.

For my father
B. P. R. Vithal
In celebration of his ninetieth

Contents

Introduction

At an interaction with students at a university near Delhi, in the winter of 2015, I asked the audience what the year 1991 meant to them. A young man replied without hesitation, and to laughter all around, 'I was born that year!'

I suggested that something else may also have happened that year. Few hazarded a reply.

Earlier that year, addressing a meeting of the Hyderabad Management Association, I had asked my middle-aged audience the same question. Many were quick to reply. It was the year in which the government had introduced new economic policies that opened up the Indian economy.

So who was responsible for that, I asked my Hyderabad audience.

'Manmohan Singh!' said many, without hesitation.

True, Manmohan Singh was the finance minister who read out the famous budget speech on 24 July 1991—one that contained several important policy initiatives and defined a new framework for India's macroeconomic policy. He became the face of the new turn in India's economic policies and played a key role as the voice of reform and liberalization even in areas for which he was not directly responsible as minister of finance.

But what was the really historic thing that happened that day, I persisted, for which Manmohan Singh was not directly responsible? Some did murmur 'decontrol' and 'delicensing'. True, the new industrial policy was not part of Singh's famous budget speech. In an initiative characteristic of Prime Minister P.V. Narasimha Rao's low-key style, the historic dismantling of the infamous 'licence-permit raj' (also called licence-permit-quota raj) had happened earlier that day when a 'statement on industrial policy' was tabled in Parliament by the minister of state for industry. It was the little known P. J. Kurien, junior minister for industry (made famous more recently by his appearance on television chairing rambunctious sessions of the Rajya Sabha), who had the privilege of tabling the historic statement that liberated Indian industry from years of what amounted to 'bureaucratic socialism'.

So, who was the senior cabinet minister for industry responsible for this major shift in India's industrial policy? Complete silence. Then someone from the back of the auditorium once again said, 'Manmohan Singh.' Wrong.

'Chidambaram!' said a few. 'Kamal Nath,' ventured some others.

On that monsoon day in Hyderabad in 2015, no one could recall that a long-time inhabitant of that city, Pamulaparthi Venkata Narasimha Rao, PV as he was always known to the Telugus, was in fact the author of the most radical shift in India's economic policy since Jawaharlal Nehru's famous Industrial Policy Resolution of 1956. Nehru's resolution had declared that India would strive to establish a 'socialistic pattern of society'. In 1991 PV moved away from that pattern to unleash private enterprise.

It is significant, and relevant to our argument about PV's centrality to the reform process, that as prime minister he not only retained the industries portfolio but also kept the Ministry of Civil Supplies and Public Distribution under his charge.

The now famous national rural employment guarantee programme (NREGA) had its initial launch during PV's tenure as prime minister.

This book is not just about PV. It is in fact about 1991. We cannot understand 1991 without understanding the role of the political leadership that made the policy changes of 1991 possible. In that fateful year, India saw new political leaders emerge out of the shadows of the Delhi durbar, who set a different course for the country to follow. Equally responsible for political and economic change were global whirlwinds of various sorts. This book is an account of the politics, the economics and the geopolitics that combined to make 1991 an important year in India's recent history. But without doubt, the central character was PV. The year made him. He made the year. For India, it was a turning point.

■

If most of us recognize the major landmarks of global or national history in our lifetime 'it is not because all of us have experienced them, even been aware at the time that they were landmarks. It is because we accept the consensus that they are landmarks', wrote historian Eric Hobsbawm. For some time now the consensus within public and academic discourse has been that the year 1991 marked a turning point in contemporary Indian history. It was a landmark year.

And yet, the commonplace view is that 1991 was eventful because of an economic crisis that forced India to take a new turn in its economic policies. But 1991 was about more than just that. It was also the year in which Rajiv Gandhi was assassinated and the Soviet Union imploded. In that dark hour, a diminutive, uncharismatic Congressman rose to the occasion.

PV was India's first 'accidental' prime minister, and a path-breaking one. He took charge of the national government and restored political stability; assumed leadership of the Congress, proving that there was hope beyond the Nehru-Gandhi dynasty; pushed through significant economic reforms; and steered India through the uncharted waters of the post-Cold War world.

PV, as I shall henceforth refer to Narasimha Rao, not only ruled a full term but his policies ushered in a new era and gave new direction to national politics. He was an unlikely prime minister but a seminal one. Unlike the many short-lived prime ministers before him—Gulzarilal Nanda (May-June 1964, 11-24 January 1966), Morarji Desai (March 1977-July 1979), Charan Singh (July 1979-January 1980), Vishwanath Pratap Singh (December 1989-November 1990) and Chandra Shekhar (November 1990-June 1991)—PV was not even a Member of Parliament on the day he was named India's twelfth prime minister.

By the summer of 1990 PV was preparing to go into retirement from public life and had packed his bags to move home to Hyderabad when circumstances catapulted him into the country's top job. This happened in a year of multiple changes and challenges for the country. India and the world were in turmoil and grappling with change, the historical significance of which was not immediately understood by many.

The economic crisis of 1991—an external payments, or a balance of payments crisis, to be precise—was in fact the consequence of a political impasse India found itself in. A series of political and economic events of the 1980s came to a head around 1990-91. India was on the verge of defaulting on its external payments obligations, with foreign exchange reserves dwindling rapidly as oil prices went up, exports went down and non-resident Indians began withdrawing their deposits in foreign currency accounts in India.

While this situation can, in part, be attributed to unexpected and extraneous factors like the Gulf War of 1990-91, one important reason for the precipitous fall in foreign exchange reserves was a loss of confidence in the Indian government's ability to deal with a difficult economic situation. That difficulty was almost entirely on account of the political brinkmanship and populism of a variety of political actors. In the end, it was politics that trumped economics.

The economic crisis of 1991 was as much a consequence of bad economic management of the preceding half decade during the tenures of Rajiv Gandhi (1984-1989) and V. P. Singh, as it was of the political choices they made. That is, the responsibility for the events that combined to push India to the brink of default must lie with Rajiv Gandhi and V. P. Singh. It was then left to Chandra Shekhar and Narasimha Rao to arrest the slide and clean up the mess. And the credit for understanding the seriousness of the situation and acting in time must go to the two of them.

It fell to a quintessential Nehruvian like PV to launch what may be best described as the post-Nehruvian era in Indian politics and foreign policy—an era which saw the country move forward in a new direction. This move away from Nehruvian economics had started during Indira Gandhi's time. She was the author of the so-called 'licence-permit raj', of sweeping nationalization, including of foreign companies, and restrictions on the growth of firms with a view to curbing the 'concentration of economic power', as it was described. Her son Rajiv Gandhi began the process of dismantling her legacy on the economic front by opening spaces for the freer play of private enterprise. However, the fact that

Nehru was succeeded in office by his daughter and grandson meant that they stayed within the framework of 'Nehruvianism'.

■

Nehruvianism, so to speak, was represented by three pillars: self-reliance, a mixed economy and non-alignment. The idea of a mixed economy was intrinsically linked to that of self-reliance given the small size and relative underdevelopment of Indian private enterprise at the time of Independence. It was not just that Nehru was inspired by the experience of rapid industrialization in the Soviet Union and by the teachings of Fabian socialism that he was taught as a student in England. Nehru was also pragmatic.

At Independence, the Congress was internally divided on economic policy, as on many other issues. While Mahatma Gandhi represented one extreme, with his views on a self-sufficient village economy and the khadi-charkha model of development, the Congress socialists were impressed by the Soviet Union's state-led model of heavy industries development. A vibrant debate ensued within the ideologically diverse Congress on what model of development India ought to follow. Nehru himself adopted an intermediate position, emphasizing the primacy of the state in industrialization but acknowledging the role of private enterprise, especially in agriculture, as well as in the manufacturing and services sectors.

He would have shared the outlook of India's business leaders that for the Indian private sector to grow and stand on its feet, it needed government support and public investment in social and economic infrastructure. This view was best articulated by a group of eminent business leaders, led by J. R. D. Tata, G. D. Birla and Purushottamdas Thakurdas, in a document titled

A Brief Memorandum Outlining a Plan of Economic Development for India. Popularly known as the 'Bombay Plan', it was published in 1945. This prescient plan called for public investment in industry, infrastructure, health and education. The public sector, it said, should enter areas of vital importance to development but only where private enterprise was either unable or unwilling to invest. All other economic activity could be left to domestic private enterprise. Through the means of a mixed economy India would become self-reliant and no longer caught up in a subordinate relationship with the developed West.

Nehru's view was best captured in the Industrial Policy Resolutions of 1948 and 1956, which acknowledged that 'the State has to assume direct responsibility for the future development of industries over a wide area'. While the policy statement went on to define the sectors where the government would be the dominant player, it also reassured private enterprise that the development of 'all the remaining industries...will be undertaken ordinarily through the initiative and enterprise of the private sector...' While Nehruvians defined this combination of socialism and capitalism as a 'mixed economy', Marxist critics dubbed it 'state capitalism' and free market critics labelled it 'bureaucratic socialism'.

The third pillar of Nehruvianism, perhaps the most enduring and the one still identified personally with Nehru, is his foreign policy of non-alignment. Post-Independence foreign policy was defined by the imperatives of post-colonial economic development as well as the choices offered by post-War global power balances. India chose to 'walk on two legs' as it were—on the one hand, befriending nations that would partner its development and, on the other, steering away from Cold War military alliances while championing the cause of other post-colonial developing countries.

In his tribute to Jawaharlal Nehru, a few months after Nehru passed away, political scientist Rajni Kothari argued that Nehru's greatest contribution to nation-building was 'not to have started a revolution but to have given rise to a consensus'. He called it 'the Congress system'. The Congress, he said, was a 'party of consensus'—an umbrella party containing within itself a wide range of interests and opinions from across the Indian subcontinent.

While the Indian national movement had within it political strands that were ideologically to the 'left' and 'right' of the Congress, and the Congress itself comprised members with varied and conflicting ideologies, the leadership of the Indian National Congress (INC) always sought to function on the basis of a consensus. It was only Mahatma Gandhi who had the moral authority to force his point of view on the organization. The rest, including Nehru and Sardar Vallabhbhai Patel, had to learn to take everyone along. As prime minister, Nehru had no option but to work with colleagues in his council of ministers who had very different views on economic, social and foreign policy.

However, both Nehru and Patel underscored the central role of the national government in defining India's post-colonial identity. The legacy of the national movement and of the politics of nation-building was such that it reinforced the idea of the centrality of the Congress to national life. In government, the Congress managed to monopolize political power as well as economic power through instruments of patronage and institutions of development.

The 'Congress system' survived Nehru's rule but not in its entirety. The rise of non-Congress parties, the successive splits within the Congress and Indira Gandhi's personalized style of leadership altered the nature of India's governing coalition, especially after 1972, when she managed to marginalize many of her opponents within the Congress and acquire undisputed power as party president and prime minister.

During the 1960s and the early 1970s, many of the 'internal' factions that defined the 'Congress system' became externalized with the creation of new parties representing specific castes and regions. The Congress remained an umbrella party but its leadership became increasingly centralized and, finally, feudalized with the emergence of the Nehru-Gandhi family as the custodians of an increasingly atrophied party. From 1972 to 1991, the Nehru-Gandhi family dominated the Congress. When some senior leaders ousted Indira after she lost power in the elections of 1977, she created a new party that came to be known as the 'Indira Congress'. She chose the 'hand' as the new party's symbol. She actively facilitated the political rise of her sons, Sanjay and Rajiv, and left no one in doubt that after her time, Rajiv should be the one to lead the party and head a future government.

All this suddenly changed when Rajiv Gandhi was assassinated in May 1991 and no family member was in a position to succeed him. The Congress was forced to walk a new path.

As Congress prime ministers, both PV and Manmohan Singh established their leadership by practising the politics of consensus. That their governments lasted their full terms in office is a testimony to their success as consensual leaders. While their economic and foreign policies were a departure from Nehru's, their style of functioning was very Nehruvian.

PV preferred the term 'middle way' or the 'path of moderation', which eschewed extremes. It most resembled the path to enlightenment set out by the Buddha. Delivering the presidential address at the Tirupati session of the All India Congress Committee (AICC) in April 1992, PV repeatedly quoted Nehru to defend his own departure from many of the central premises of Nehruvian economic policy.

> To interpret Nehru's middle way as being valid only in a bipolar situation is not to understand our ancient philosophy of the Middle Way. The Middle Way was meant to be a constant reminder that no assertion or its opposite can be the full and complete truth. It meant that we looked for Truth in the interstices of dogmas. It means today that we will accept no dogma even if it happens to be the only dogma remaining in the field at a given moment. Our quest for Truth will still continue.

■

India's first non-Congress government was, in fact, a coalition headed by a former Congressman, Morarji Desai, and included several Congress leaders who had parted company with Indira Gandhi after she imposed Emergency rule in the summer of 1975. The Indian Constitution allows the central government to assume dictatorial powers in the event of an 'emergency'—if the security of a part or all of India is threatened by 'war or external aggression or armed rebellion'. When the Gandhian leader Jayaprakash Narayan urged security forces to disobey the 'anti-people' orders of the elected government, he gave the politically beleaguered Indira Gandhi the opportunity to impose Emergency rule. In the general elections of 1977 the Indira Congress was down to 153 MPs in the Lok Sabha and the Janata alliance secured 298 seats.

Formed in 1977, that government saw a change of prime minister even before it settled down. Another ex-Congressman, Charan Singh, who had quit the Congress as a critic of Nehru and had launched the Bharatiya Lok Dal, replaced Desai as prime minister in July 1979. That unstable government too soon came apart and was defeated in the mid-term elections of January 1980. Indira Gandhi returned to power in 1980 and was assassinated in 1984. Her brutal assassination in her own home by her own bodyguards resulted in a tsunami wave of sympathy that delivered 404 seats to the Congress under Rajiv Gandhi.

In October 1988, V. P. Singh, a senior minister, quit Rajiv Gandhi's government, accusing him of corruption in defence procurement deals, and formed the Janata Dal, merging elements from the Janata Party that was in power in 1977-79, some former Congress members and the Lok Dal party. Rajiv was wounded by the corruption charges. The case related to the distribution of commissions to various individuals by the Swedish defence equipment manufacturer, Bofors. It was widely believed that one of the beneficiaries, an Italian businessman, Ottavio Quattrocchi, was a friend of Sonia Gandhi's. Rajiv Gandhi's less than impressive record as prime minister and the charges of corruption levelled against him by his former colleagues contributed to a precipitous fall in the party's vote share, by over 10 percentage points, and the party won only 197 seats in the Lok Sabha in the general election of 1989.

Once again, in 1989, a group of former Congress members joined hands with non-Congress parties to form yet another short-lived coalition. After the defeat of the Indira Congress, V. P. Singh headed India's second coalition government with the outside support of the Bharatiya Janata Party (BJP) and the Communist parties. V. P. Singh declared that the time of single party governments had passed and that India had entered the 'era of coalitions'.

V. P. Singh's government was riven by rivalries from day one. Singh first proposed the name of Haryana leader Devi Lal to ensure that party veteran Chandra Shekhar would not become prime minister, and then stepped in when Devi Lal withdrew his candidature in favour of Singh. Devi Lal was made deputy prime minster as part of the deal.

A livid Chandra Shekhar conspired to oust Singh from the outset. He was helped in this effort by parties that had initially supported the Janata Dal but began having second thoughts. Thus the BJP withdrew support due to differences on the issue of building a temple to Lord Rama at Ayodhya in Uttar Pradesh. Singh's popularity among the urban middle classes, gained through his campaign against corruption, dissipated when he chose to extend the scope of reservations in educational institutions and government for social groups classified as 'Other Backward Classes (OBC)'—that is 'other than' the Scheduled Castes and Scheduled Tribes (SC and ST) who enjoy constitutional protection for educational and employment reservations.

Singh's government lost parliamentary majority in October 1990—after less than a full year in office—and Chandra Shekhar formed yet another minority government with the outside support of the Congress Party. That government too had to quit in March 1991.

Through all of this there was increasing trouble within the Congress. Through the winter of 1990-91, political reporters and analysts writing about the Congress Party for the *Economic Times*, where I was an assistant editor, reported on the growing frustration and factionalism within a dispirited Congress Party. After the Congress's historic victory of 1984, when in the aftermath of Indira's assassination it won 404 seats in the 514-member Lok

Sabha, it faced the ignominy of winning just 197 seats in 1989. Within five years the party's vote share had plummeted from over 49 per cent of votes polled to around 39 per cent.

The party's seniors and regional satraps began to realize that Rajiv was no Indira. Indira had brought the party back to power in 1980 after being trounced in 1977. Rajiv and his Doon School friends showed no such political acumen, having squandered the unprecedented mandate of 1984.

In a hard-hitting column published in January 1990 in the left-wing magazine *Mainstream,* and written by someone identified mysteriously as a 'Congressman', Rajiv Gandhi's 'style of functioning' was severely criticized and the decline in the Congress's political standing was attributed to the growing distance between the party's political base and its increasingly elitist leadership.

> The momentum of the 1984 election verdict would have normally lasted for two, even three terms, perpetuating Rajiv Gandhi's leadership (in his own right, not as Indira's son) for a long spell such as his grandfather's and mother's. But that was not to be... The meteoric rise plummeted to virtual zero some time in 1987—at about mid-term. Thereafter the hero of young India became almost a source of derisive entertainment to kids in a million homes.

Many have come to believe that the writer was none other than P. V. Narasimha Rao. While *Mainstream*'s founder-editor, the late Nikhil Chakravartty, refused to divulge the name during his lifetime, PV's biographer, Vinay Sitapati, believes the mysterious Congressman was indeed PV.

In the summer of 1991, following Rajiv Gandhi's assassination and PV's elevation as party president, PV was invited by President

R. Venkataraman to form the government. His minority government managed to remain in office for a year and a half before securing a parliamentary majority. 1991 thus marked a turning point between the era of Congress Party dominance and the era of more enduring coalitions that followed. After a series of short-lived coalitions, PV ensured that a Congress government headed by a non-Nehru-Gandhi remained in office for a full term. Since then the Congress has had to remain content being part of a coalition, albeit the dominant partner.

Even as the dark clouds of the external payments crisis gathered through the second half of 1990 and early 1991, nothing but short-term political considerations and extreme political cynicism shaped the priorities of political parties at home. Each political player—the Indira Congress, Janata Dal, BJP, the Left Front (led by the Communist Party of India [Marxist]) and the regional parties—was only interested in government formation and the spoils of office. Issues ranging from the extension of reservations in educational institutions and government jobs to new social groups, the construction of a temple for Lord Rama on the site of the Babri Masjid in Ayodhya, corruption in defence equipment procurement, legal protection for Muslim women and so on occupied the attention of most political leaders. Hardly anyone paid attention to the deteriorating external payments situation.

■

Like the shift away from the Congress system in political management, the turn away from Nehruvian economics to what one may rightfully describe as 'Narasimhanomics' occurred through several gradual moves, beginning with Indira Gandhi's decision to enter into a borrowing programme with the International

Monetary Fund (IMF) in 1981. This shift gained pace during Rajiv Gandhi's tenure in the 1980s.

However, Indira Gandhi was defensive and tentative in the policy reform she chose to undertake after 1980. She made much of returning the last tranche of the IMF loan and ending the programme when faced with criticism from the Communist parties. Her modest attempt to change course would always be viewed against the radicalism of many of her earlier policies. In fact, the licence-permit raj and many restrictions on business enterprise were post-Nehruvian and the contribution of Indira Gandhi. Rajiv Gandhi too was defensive in his liberalization moves, not wanting to be viewed as pro-business. As the economist Jagdish Bhagwati observed, '[Rajiv Gandhi's] reforms were hardly revolutionary in conception or in execution. In retrospect, they amounted to an acquiescence in the regime but a mild attempt at moderating its worst excesses.'

PV was unabashed about his moves. The 'credibility' of his initiative, as Bhagwati notes, was 'far greater'. He was convinced that the ancien régime (the licence-permit raj) must go. And that is what he made happen. Within a month of taking charge PV dismantled it in one fell swoop. Indian enterprise, PV believed, would bloom if liberated from the straitjacket of bureaucratic socialism. It is worth noting that he was the only prime minister who had the political courage to confer a business leader with the nation's highest honour, when he bestowed the Bharat Ratna on J. R. D. Tata. No businessman has since been so honoured.

■

The world watched with concern the drift in India's domestic politics at a time of mounting economic and global uncertainty.

The country's balance of payments, already under stress thanks to rising oil prices and falling exports, came under further pressure when international credit rating agencies placed India under watch, concerned about the country's economic and political capacity to service high external debt, especially short-term debt.

India's sovereign credit ratings had gone up and down over the years but never before had any rating agency pointed to 'political risk' as a reason for downgrading India. That happened in October 1990. In December 1990 Chandra Shekhar committed his government to implementing policies that could have averted a balance of payments crisis. His finance minister, Yashwant Sinha, entered into a fiscal stabilization and structural adjustment programme with the IMF. If he had been allowed to present his government's budget in February 1991, and undertake the reforms the government had promised the IMF it would, confidence in India would have been restored. That did not happen.

The global environment too was in a flux. The end of the Cold War and the implosion of the Soviet Union had altered the strategic environment shaping Indian foreign policy. China, for a long time a dragon asleep, or at least one with its head hidden between its legs and looking inward, was emerging as a more open and dynamic economy. Asia to India's east was rapidly moving ahead, while Asia to India's west was embroiled in conflict. The delicate balance of power in West Asia was rudely disturbed when Iraq's Saddam Hussein invaded Kuwait. India felt the impact of this destabilization as oil prices shot up.

At around the same time the global trading system underwent a transformation with the General Agreement on Tariffs and Trade (GATT) being replaced by the World Trade Organization (WTO). The WTO created a new multilateral trading system with a set of disciplines that allowed member governments to seek legal recourse for the settlement of trade disputes. Taken together, a new global regime of strategic and economic relations impacted India.

∎

Marking the silver jubilee of PV's assumption of office as prime minister, and his implementation of economic reforms, dozens of essays have been written during the past few months of 2016 by economic policy analysts. The story that most economists like to tell is that in 1991 good economics drove out bad economics. Few have made the point that in that historic year, good politics also drove out bad politics. By good politics I mean good political management. PV's wisdom came to India's rescue. The brinkmanship, the one-upmanship, the short-termism of the 1989-91 period, driven by the petty political ambitions of myopic and inexperienced leaders, was replaced by a long-term vision of a long distance runner. True, Chandra Shekhar too could have been India's man of destiny. But destiny chose PV.

Most informed Indians think only of the economic crisis and its management when they even care to remember what 1991 was all about. It would seem that a vast majority among those who can recall that 1991 was the year of economic liberalization still do not know the role played by PV. Very few can readily recall the political and foreign policy challenges that PV had to deal with and, much less, PV's imprint on the policies pursued.

I have often been asked how one should evaluate the tenure of a prime minister. My reply has always been that one must compare the nation, the polity and the economy that a person inherits the day she takes charge with the state of affairs when one demits that office. By that yardstick Jawaharlal Nehru was a great prime minister at the end of his first decade in office. His image and legacy were dented by the last five years of his tenure, especially the border war with China in 1962. Indira Gandhi entered the history books by supporting the struggle for the liberation of Bangladesh. But her management of the economy was patchy. All the prime ministers who had short-lived tenures during the 1960s, 1970s and 1980s and Rajiv Gandhi did not leave the kind of imprint that would earn them a place in the history books. PV did. He steered the country through a period of political uncertainty, economic crisis and shift in the global balance of power.

The initiatives that PV took within a year of assuming office have since defined the post-Nehruvian era in India. The policy shift on the economic front was the more obvious of the changes and the one that has received the most academic attention. Less appreciated have been the shifts on the foreign policy front, both within Asia and around the world, and the interrelationship between the two. Finally, there was the new turn on the political front with the era of single party dominance giving way to an era of coalitions.

As I have noted, India's political leadership had to deal with multiple changes and challenges, at home and abroad, in the context of a most difficult balance of payments and fiscal crisis. The man of the moment was Prime Minister Narasimha Rao. The manner in which PV dealt with each of these challenges marks 1991 as a 'landmark' year, to use Hobsbawm's term. After 1947 it was, without doubt, the single most important year in India's contemporary history.

In keeping with the book's argument that it was politics that trumped economics in 1991, within a particular global context, we will begin our narrative with an account of how a war in West Asia cast its shadow both on the politics and economics of 1991. We will then discuss the nature of the economic crisis and its resolution. Next we will examine how the stabilization of the economy helped stabilize the polity and initiated a new direction on the economic and political front. The 'Indira Congress' once again became the Indian National Congress at the 1992 Tirupati session of the AICC. The party briefly came out of the long shadow of the Nehru-Gandhis. Finally, we look at PV's legacy against the background of changes at home and those sweeping the world.

The story of 1991 begins with external events impacting India. Through the spring, summer and monsoon months, domestic economics and politics shaped the course of events. In the winter of 1991 tectonic shifts in the global balance of power altered India's strategic environment.

India entered 1991 with trepidation. As the year came to an end it found its feet.

Chapter 1

January: The Politics

In the early hours of 9 January 1991, a giant United States Air Force's transport aircraft, the C-141 Starlifter, lowered its body onto the tarmac of Bombay's Sahar International Airport (now called Chhatrapati Shivaji International Airport). While on a flight from a US airbase in the Philippines to a base in the Gulf the aircraft decided to refuel in Bombay. Operation Desert Storm, the US attack on Iraq, aimed at liberating Kuwait from Saddam Hussein's occupation army, was about to be launched. The US armed forces were gathering men and material in countries surrounding Iraq in preparation for an attack.

Information of the aircraft's arrival and departure was conveyed by the Intelligence Bureau to the then cabinet secretary, Naresh Chandra. Chandra decided that the prime minister should be briefed immediately. Prime Minister Chandra Shekhar, an ex-Congressman and a quintessential Congress socialist, was angry. Why would the United States want to implicate India in its campaign against Iraq's strongman, Saddam Hussein? Saddam had been friendly towards India, the only Arab leader to support India against Pakistan on the Kashmir issue. But then Chandra reminded the prime minister that Saddam had now become a

terrible dictator, ready to destroy any opposition. He had become
unpopular among the Arabs and was engaged in a territorial
dispute with Iran. Moreover, India needed US support in securing
assistance from the IMF. It was time for India to rethink its
approach.

Chandra Shekhar had attained political fame as a Congress
radical—a leader of the 'young Turks' as they came to be known
for rebelling against the political conservatism of the party's old
guard after Jawaharlal Nehru passed away. He quit the Congress
Party in protest against Indira Gandhi's decision to perpetuate
herself in office by imposing the Emergency and suspending
the normal functioning of a democratic Constitution. In 1977,
he joined forces with such known critics of Nehru and Indira
as Jayaprakash Narayan and Morarji Desai to form the Janata
Party. When the Janata Party came to power in 1977, he chose
to be party president rather than become a minister in Morarji's
Cabinet. He may well have viewed Morarji, already eighty-one,
as a transitional figure. Still only fifty and now party president,
he thought he would achieve greater political success if he were
thought of as a successor to the octogenarian prime minister.
Spartan in lifestyle, Chandra Shekhar had learnt how power
worked in Lutyens Delhi. By 1990 he had come to be viewed
as a pragmatic nationalist.

The foreign office was, however, divided on Iraq. Some felt
Saddam was still a useful friend of India and so the government
should deny refuelling facilities to US military aircraft henceforth.
Others felt that Saddam's actions had already imposed a heavy
burden on India not only by pushing oil prices up but also by
creating uncertainty for thousands of Indians living in Kuwait.
Moreover, there was no evidence that the aircraft that had already

refuelled and left was carrying any military hardware. It, and those to follow, may have had only non-combat materiel.

Even though India was a non-aligned nation during the Cold War, it had reached out to the US for military assistance when attacked by China in 1962, and to the Soviet Union in 1971, in preparation for the liberation of Bangladesh (when the US and China had ganged up on Pakistan's side). It was now India's turn to respond to a US request for help.

Chandra Shekhar's major concern at the time, apart from ensuring the political survival of his minority government, was to get the IMF to extend balance of payments support to India. India's foreign exchange reserves were rapidly dwindling, and it had thus approached the IMF, the lender of last resort, in December 1990. The United States was the largest shareholder on the IMF board, and in that capacity had virtual veto power when it came to the authorization of loans. The US could hurt India by not supporting its loan application.

Back in 1981 the US had threatened to do just that when Indira Gandhi's government approached the IMF for a US$5 billion extended fund facility. At that time, the US wanted more forthright criticism of the Soviet invasion of Afghanistan than what Indira Gandhi had been willing to make. Not that Indira was not critical of the Soviets. When the Russian supremo, Leonid Brezhnev, asked Indira, 'I want to get out of Afghanistan. Please show me the way,' she is reported to have said, in a tone that implied disapproval, 'The way out is the same as the way in.'

The US sought a more public condemnation of the Soviets. But India still needed the Soviets, not least because they were still the most important suppliers of defence equipment. The rupee-rouble trade also made USSR an important trade partner, with a share of over 16 per cent in India's total trade. India's executive director on the IMF board, M. Narasimham, was advised to tell the Americans that if the US did not support India's application then India's dependence on the Comecon (Council for Mutual Economic Assistance), a Soviet-led economic grouping including socialist economies and the allies of the Soviets, would only increase.

But a decade later, in 1991, that threat held no water. The Cold War had ended, the Soviet Union was still around but was gradually disintegrating and the Comecon had little economic heft. India needed dollars.

The prime minister turned to President Venkataraman for advice. The president advised Chandra Shekhar to play ball with the Americans. No doubt Venkataraman was aware of how the world had changed and also had in mind the changing dynamics of US-India relations.

As US strategic policy guru Henry Kissinger explained in a column in the *India Today*, the purpose of the US intervention in the Gulf was not to dethrone Saddam, but to ensure that no one country emerged as a regional hegemon in the new post-Cold War world. Whatever the merits of US strategy, the fact is that Saddam's invasion of Kuwait gave the US an early opportunity to define the new rules of engagement in the emerging post-Cold War world. India understood the game in time.

Venkataraman was an experienced political figure. He had been minister for finance, home affairs and defence in Indira Gandhi's Cabinet in the early 1980s. Along with PV and Pranab Mukherjee, Venkataraman had been considered prime ministerial material even during Indira's time. After the controversial, and dubious, tenure of Giani Zail Singh as president, Venkataraman was viewed as a textbook president. Zail Singh thrived on politicking. He remained a provincial politician dabbling in the increasingly messy politics of the Punjab even as he occupied the palace of the president. Venkataraman was statesmanlike. He came to play a critical role in managing India's many problems in 1991, as we shall see later.

Cabinet Secretary Chandra too lent his weight to the view that India could not afford to displease the US at a time when it was seeking financial support from the IMF and the World Bank. His view mattered. Naresh Chandra was the quintessential civil servant in the mould of the old Indian Civil Service, and played the part of cabinet secretary to the hilt. Tall and big built, he exuded authority and supreme confidence as the senior-most civil servant of the government. He was the kind of person who would allow his boss—in this case none other than the prime minister—to sleep in peace knowing that his government was in competent hands. Candid and precise in his advice, Chandra could also quote rule and precedent to back his views. Yet, his sense of humour and good-natured 'arre bhai' would immediately put his interlocutors at ease.

Chandra Shekhar trusted the cabinet secretary's judgement. He chose to remain quiet. The US aircraft were only landing to buy fuel, and this was permissible under international law. The only minor concession India had to extend was to forgo checking the cargo aboard the aircraft and take the declaration in the manifest as factual. The declaration did not list any military hardware or troops on board. But who knew what was inside? The government did not insist on entering the craft to check what was on board. That was a conscious decision of the prime minister and his cabinet secretary. Chandra Shekhar's helpful 'pragmatism' did not go unnoticed in Washington DC.

Over the next month, two US military aircraft landed every day at the Bombay, Madras and Agra airports, flying from the Philippines to the Gulf. Bombay's Sahar airport and Madras's Nungambakkam airport were civilian airports. Agra was a military airport. Moreover, Madras and Bombay can be regarded to be on a straight line from the Philippines to the Gulf. Agra was further north. Perhaps the fact that India allowed US military aircraft to land at a military airfield was in itself seen as an important gesture. The US also sought and secured transit facilities for its navy. On 21 January, the USS *Ford*, a guided missile frigate, docked at the Bombay harbour, also en route from the Pacific to the Gulf.

For over two weeks these visits remained unreported. On 28 January 1991, the *Times of India* 'spilled some hazardous beans', as Inder Kumar Gujral, V. P. Singh's foreign minister, observed in his autobiography. It was Gujral who had originally authorized the overflight of US military aircraft over Indian territory. He claims he had done so during peace time with no knowledge of any planned US attack on Iraq. Gujral had been severely criticized at home for hugging Saddam Hussein in a warm gesture of friendship even as Indian workers in Kuwait were living in fear of invading Iraqi soldiers.

The news of the government's decision to permit overflight by US military aircraft broke around the same time that the IMF sanctioned its US$1.8 billion support to India. The incident brought into sharp relief India's own reassessment of changing global geopolitical balances. It also demonstrated how closely India's economic and foreign policy choices and domestic politics had become intertwined in the January of 1991.

Once the media became aware of the decision, the anti-US and pro-Saddam voices in the country demanded an end to refuelling. Some political parties objected. Some columnists criticized the government. Not much else happened. Chandra Shekhar dismissed these objections and continued to allow US military aircraft to land at Indian airports till the third week of February.

It was not surprising that many in India and around the world viewed the Chandra Shekhar government's decision to permit refuelling of US military planes as a political concession aimed at securing US support for an IMF loan. It was also thought of as an early Indian response to the shift underway in the global balance of power with the fall of the Berlin Wall in 1989. Indian defence strategists were also aware that China had become militarily active in the Gulf, with growing defence ties to Iraq and Saudi Arabia. India could not afford to sit back on its haunches.

Years later, the foreign secretary of the day, Muchkund Dubey, would confirm this to a Korean scholar, stating that this decision, a change from existing policy, 'was deliberately and consciously introduced in order to meet the challenge of the post-Cold War situation. It was clearly realized that after the Cold War, United States has emerged as the only superpower. It was felt that it was important to deal with the United States without the blinkers of ideology which used to be the case before.'

But the US administration wasn't the only entity Prime Minister Chandra Shekhar had to keep happy that January. He had to keep the president of the Congress Party happy too. Remember, the prime minister was heading a minority government with the support of the Congress. His Janata Party had a mere 64 members in the 529-member Lok Sabha, and he needed the support of Rajiv Gandhi's 197 Congress MPs.

It wasn't that Rajiv did not understand the importance of growing US–India defence cooperation, particularly following his successful visit to Washington DC in 1985. In December 1990, President George Bush Sr. sent his assistant secretary of defence for international security, Henry Rowen, to New Delhi along with a large delegation of civil and military officials. While the US was looking at India as a potential partner in dealing with a resurgent China and a troublesome West Asia, India was viewing the US as a source of both technology and defence cooperation given the declining fortunes of the Soviet Union, the rise of China and the problems with Pakistan.

But larger and long-term strategic issues were hardly on Rajiv's mind; he had his own problems. Within two months of extending Congress's support to Chandra Shekhar to form a government, he realized his folly. Chandra Shekhar had become a bigger problem than Rajiv could ever imagine. He was, after all, a former Congressman from Indira's days and knew the Congress well. Rajiv suspected that Chandra Shekhar was getting together with powerful provincial Congress leaders like Sharad Pawar to lengthen the longevity of his minority government. He may have hoped to lure the Congress Party, in spite of Rajiv, to join a coalition government. He had Rajiv and his coterie at sixes and sevens.

■

Seized of the fact that the economy was in bad shape and needed urgent attention, Chandra Shekhar invited I. G. Patel to take charge as finance minister. Patel declined, opting for a quiet retired life in Baroda.

Dr Indraprasad Gordhanbhai Patel, IG to those who knew

him well, was an economist with a stellar reputation and years of experience in both the central government and international financial institutions. While IG was regarded by his peers as a thorough professional, the fact that he was from Gujarat and had worked directly under Morarji Desai, a fellow Gujarati, during Desai's long innings as finance minister in Nehru's and Indira's governments, may have made Indira Gandhi regard him as 'Morarji's man', as IG himself puts it in his autobiography. In 1972, after Indira's politics had moved to the left and her relations with Morarji deteriorated further, IG moved to New York to join the United Nations Development Programme (UNDP). When Morarji became prime minister in 1977, he invited IG to return to become the Governor of the Reserve Bank of India (RBI). Such was his credibility that when Indira Gandhi returned to power, in 1980, she allowed IG to complete the remainder of his five-year term at the central bank. In fact, in 1981, he was actively associated with India's approach to the IMF for an extended financing facility (EFF) loan.

Soft-spoken, dapper and with an interest in the arts and music, IG was a renaissance man. He related with equal ease to fellow economists, civil service colleagues and politicians of all hues. Despite his long years in government he retained an academic's curiosity and easy way of dealing with younger people. As director of the Indian Institute of Management-Ahmedabad (IIM-A; 1982-84) and later as director of the London School of Economics and Political Science (1984-90), IG was very popular with his students. Despite his own mainstream conservative outlook, he was always encouraging of young students with radical views.

In January 1991, when I first learnt of Chandra Shekhar's invitation to IG, I interviewed IG for the *Economic Times* and asked

him why he had declined the post. He evaded a direct reply and
requested that I not write about it, saying, 'It would not be helpful
for anyone if you wrote about it.' He knew that such a news
report would embarrass an already beleaguered prime minister.
I had to rest content just mentioning the fact that I had asked
IG about Chandra Shekhar's invitation to take over as finance
minister and that he neither confirmed nor denied the rumour.

Even as IG declined the offer, economist-turned-politician
Subramanian Swamy pressed his claim for the North Block job.
However, Chandra Shekhar named Swamy minister for commerce
and appointed Yashwant Sinha, a former civil servant who had
quit the Indian Administrative Service to get elected to Parliament,
as finance minister. Sinha's preference was for external affairs but
he readily agreed to wear the crown of thorns. His entry into
the Ministry of Finance was baptism by fire.

■

Earlier, on 6 December 1990, about a month after the Chandra
Shekhar government was formed, I was in the US to speak at
a conference on India at the University of Texas in Austin. On
my way home, I spent a couple of days in Washington DC. I
decided to call on India's executive director on the IMF board,
Gopi Arora, to get his assessment of the economic situation in
India and how the IMF was viewing it. Arora had been an
influential official in the Indira and Rajiv Gandhi governments.
He invited me to join him for lunch at the IMF headquarters.
When I reached his office, his secretary let me into his room,
saying Arora was expecting me.

As soon as I entered the room, the two gentlemen seated
with Arora gasped on seeing me, a journalist. Arora's visitors were

C. Rangarajan, deputy governor of the RBI and Deepak Nayyar, chief economic adviser to the Government of India. They were on a secret mission to the IMF in search of balance of payments support. Arora feigned ignorance of my media affiliation. He said he knew me as Vithal's son and his son's teacher—Arora's son, Ashish, had been a student at the Jawaharlal Nehru University the year I had taught there, in the mid-1980s.

The JNU connection also explains my friendship with Deepak. We had been colleagues on the faculty of the Centre for Economic Studies and Planning. Nayyar inhabited the two very different worlds of academia and government with equal ease and aplomb. He had taught at universities in England and India, and was a professor at IIM, Calcutta. His first stint in government was as economic adviser in the Commerce Ministry in the mid-1980s. He went back to teach at JNU only to return to government as chief economic adviser. He was always willing to spend time with journalists to educate them on government thinking on economic policy, thus endearing himself to an entire generation of economic journalists reporting on the crisis of 1990-91.

Rangarajan (who also knew my family) was just as approachable. He too began his career as an academic, teaching at IIM, Ahmedabad, and then moved to the RBI as deputy governor in the early 1980s. Working at the *Economic Times* in Delhi I could always get him on the phone when I needed to understand some aspect of policy. As I look back after twenty-five years I am convinced that the relationship of trust that many in key economic policy roles had built with the media contributed to the government's management of the crisis.

The three gentlemen sat me down and made me promise that I would not breathe a word to anyone about the meeting

I had chanced upon. I gave my word and kept it for a decade. In December 2000, at the end of ten years of silence, I shared that episode with the readers of the *Financial Express*, of which I was then chief editor.

During the course of that lunch meeting, I was told that in August 1990 Nayyar had in fact proposed to Prime Minister V. P. Singh that the government approach the IMF but PMO officials told Nayyar that the prime minister had said, 'Not yet'. Singh's decision was probably due to the fact that the situation was not as desperate as it became later, but was also a function of his dependence on the support of the Left Front parties to remain in office. The Left would surely have opposed any move to go to the IMF. Nayyar, however, was batting for an IMF loan more as a way of demonstrating to creditors that India had the IMF's support. Funding from the IMF was not just needed for the dollars it would bring in. While the money was certainly important, what was equally essential was the IMF's imprimatur: it was necessary to broadcast the perception that the world's lender of last resort was standing behind India. It was a political signal and a message to creditors and investors alike—a character certificate that would help India deal with increasingly worried creditors.

In December 1990, by which time Chandra Shekhar had taken over, India desperately needed dollars to pay for basic imports like oil and food. Chandra Shekhar's hand was initially stayed by his left wing, socialist friends and advisers like economist S. K. Goyal. However, if Goyal's ideological predilections inhibited him from advocating an approach to the IMF, the prime minister's more pragmatic economic adviser, Manmohan Singh, would have no such inhibitions. More importantly, unlike V. P. Singh, Chandra Shekhar was willing to take political risks. If IMF support was not forthcoming, he would do whatever it took to prevent default.

'If the Fund cannot extend a lifeline,' Nayyar told Michel Camdessus, the managing director of the IMF during one of the meetings during the subsequent negotiations, 'we will bring the shutters down!'

He meant that India would have to drastically curb imports—virtually banning all imports except food and oil—to save foreign exchange. The government in fact raised the cash margins on imports sharply to discourage new orders being placed. This would require importers to keep a higher share of the value of imported goods in ready cash, rather than credit.

The negotiations yielded an immediate inflow of US$1.8 billion, made available in January 1991 through a standby arrangement and the IMF's compensatory and contingency financing facility (CCFF). The latter was in part meant to offer balance of payments support to countries experiencing shortfalls in export earnings due to temporary and unforeseen factors beyond the control of member governments. India qualified for CCFF support since it was hit by a spike in oil prices caused by Iraq's invasion of Kuwait.

While extending a helping hand, the IMF drew attention to India's long-term problems. The mounting external debt situation had been made worse by the fact that the share of short-term debt had risen steeply in recent years. If India wished to avert a payment default, it would be better advised to enter into a medium-term structural adjustment and stabilization programme. Camdessus assured Rangarajan and Nayyar that increased IMF support would be available provided the Indian government was able to get its annual budget passed.

This condition had a dual implication. One, that the

government would have to prove its majority in Parliament. Under Indian law if the government's annual finance bill is rejected by the Lok Sabha, the government of the day falls. Under normal circumstances this would be a trivial condition. But the situation was not normal. Prime Minister Chandra Shekhar was still not sure if Rajiv Gandhi would allow him to present a regular budget and get it approved by Parliament. Two, the IMF would want to see some policy reform, including industrial policy and trade liberalization and reduction in the fiscal deficit through concrete measures to raise revenues, raise the price of fuel and other administered prices and curb expenditure. Politically speaking, all this was highly sensitive stuff. That would explain Rangarajan and Nayyar's reaction to my entry into Arora's room.

■

Finance Minister Sinha went to Parliament in late December 1990 to announce policy measures that would satisfy the IMF. The most important commitment he made was to cut the fiscal deficit by 2 percentage points of the GDP (gross domestic product). Only a squeeze on public spending would convince the IMF that India was serious about setting its house in order. The IMF always set conditions that borrowers had to adhere to in order to secure its support. While professional economists at the IMF would draw up a list of policy to-dos, IMF conditionalities were not always only about good economics and nor were they always stated in black and white. Member governments represented on the IMF board would have their own expectations, often conveyed through political channels. As the IMF's biggest shareholder, the United States never shied away from making both economic and political demands on debtor nations. One such test was to see if India would cooperate with the US in the Gulf War by allowing the refuelling of US military aircraft. India passed the test.

■

Chandra Shekhar's growing confidence, even though he was heading a minority government, began to worry Rajiv Gandhi. Some of his advisers were convinced that Chandra Shekhar, the old war horse, would get a section of the Congress Party to challenge Rajiv's leadership. In November 1990, after the fall of the V. P. Singh government, President Venkataraman had asked Rajiv if he would like to stake his claim, as leader of the single largest group in Parliament, to form the government. Rajiv had declined, assuring the president that the Congress would ensure political stability by supporting the Chandra Shekhar government at least for a year. The government of the day had several crises to deal with—the Mandal agitation for expanding the scope of reservations, the Mandir agitation aimed at building a temple for Lord Rama in Ayodhya, the insurgency in the Northeastern region and in Punjab, the unrest in Kashmir, the unease in Tamil Nadu following the aborted Indian attempt to help Sri Lanka eliminate the Tamil Tigers and, above all, the balance of payments crisis, with the lingering fear of an external default.

'I asked Rajiv Gandhi if his support [for the Chandra Shekhar government] would continue at least for one year,' recalls President Venkataraman. Rajiv replied, 'Why one year? It may extend to the life of Parliament.'

In his memoirs, the Nehru-Gandhi family loyalist Makhan Lal Fotedar tells us that Venkataraman despised Chandra Shekhar and did not wish to swear him in as prime minister in November 1990. Fotedar goes on to state that Venkataraman suggested to

Rajiv that the Congress seek permission to form a government under the leadership of Pranab Mukherjee.

'On this the President directed me, with an emphasis of authority, that I may put it to Rajiv Gandhi that if he supported Mr Pranab Mukherjee to be Prime Minister, he (the President) would administer the oath of office to him that same evening.'

Fotedar even claims that Venkataraman 'expressed caution against choosing Chandra Shekhar and made some adverse remarks about him'.

However, in his own autobiography, Venkataraman has a different view of Chandra Shekhar. Explaining why he chose to swear in a minority government despite his own preference for a workable coalition, Venkataraman says, 'Personally I have a high regard for Chandra Shekhar, for his rational views, progressive approach to the nation's problems and his integrity. I would have had no problem in choosing him if he had a better following than a bare tenth of the membership of the Lok Sabha.'

Through the month of January, Rajiv Gandhi kept contemplating the withdrawal of support to the government. Each time Venkataraman was informed of an imminent move to do so he would caution Rajiv 'against breaking the government and creating instability in the country'.

At one point Venkataraman asked him if he would be ready to form a government, and records in his memoirs, 'He was a real Hamlet debating "to be or not to be" a Prime Minister.'

Venkataraman's only concern was that a political crisis at that time, days before the Parliament was to meet to vote on the union budget, would have grave consequences for the economy. He wanted the budget passed by Parliament. By mid-February 1991 Rajiv Gandhi realized that allowing the government's budget to be voted on in Parliament would not just help secure an IMF loan for India, but would in fact help extend the life of the Chandra Shekhar government. As we have noted, parliamentary approval of the budget is akin to a vote of confidence. It allows a minority ruling party to remain in government till it is displaced through a vote of no-confidence in a subsequent session of Parliament. This would mean Chandra Shekhar would remain prime minister at least until the convening of the monsoon session in July. To prevent this, Rajiv first forced a delay in budget presentation. Rather than allow the budget to be presented to Parliament on the last day of February, as is the norm, Rajiv demanded and secured a postponement to 7 March.

The Congress then upped its demand by insisting on a 'vote on account'. A vote on account is a legislative device by which Parliament allows the government to continue spending so that the normal business of government can go on, and salaries are paid. The regular annual budget statement and the parliamentary approval of the 'finance bill' enables the government to legislate changes in tax policy. Through a regular budget the government can bring in new tax laws and raise additional revenue. A vote on account implies that government revenues are determined by existing tax laws. Deferring the presentation of a regular budget would also mean that no other legislative or policy business would get done and the important policy changes being demanded by the IMF would not get implemented.

■

On 5 March 1991, the *Economic Times* had a celebratory party to mark its thirtieth anniversary. An audio-visual presentation was played showing major events and personalities that made the news over the three decades since *ET*'s launch. 1961 was an eventful year. The Russian cosmonaut Yuri Gagarin became the first human in space. It was the year the Berlin Wall came up. And John F. Kennedy became President of the United States.

Nothing of such historical significance had yet happened in 1991, though parts of the world were in the throes of change and turmoil. The Berlin Wall had come down nearly a year earlier. China's economy was perking up a year after the government squashed a pro-democracy movement led by young people gathered at Beijing's Tiananmen Square. In August 1990, war had broken out once again in West Asia, and oil prices had gone up.

On that March evening it looked like it would be another year of plodding on with political and economic uncertainty in India. It was generally known that the economy was not in good health, even though government officials tried to be reassuring. In late January, speaking to Paranjoy Guha Thakurta of *India Today* magazine, Manmohan Singh, then adviser to Prime Minister Chandra Shekhar, conceded that there were concerns about the sustainability of government finances and the balance of payments, but tried to calm nerves saying, 'There is no doubt that we are going through a difficult economic situation... Despite the problems we are currently facing, the underlying health of the Indian economy is not all that bad.'

As the evening wore on, a buzz spread through the gathering of business leaders, government officials, diplomats, journalists and a variety of *ET* loyalists. The chief guest of the evening, Union Finance Minister Yashwant Sinha, had not arrived. He was delayed, we were told, as he had been urgently summoned by the prime minister. Earlier that day, Congress MPs had disrupted Parliament accusing the Chandra Shekhar government of 'snooping' on Rajiv Gandhi. A controversy had been created. Most political reporters assumed it was just one of those political tantrums aimed at showing who was boss, given that Chandra Shekhar's minority government depended on the Congress Party for survival. No one imagined that this tantrum would turn into a crisis.

'Of course the prime minister had not ordered any snooping on Rajiv,' recalls Naresh Chandra, the cabinet secretary. According to Chandra, an ambitious official of the Rajasthan cadre of the Indian Police Service, desperate for a better posting, had placed two ill-trained Haryana state police constables outside Rajiv's house to gather information that he hoped would be of some use to his political bosses in Haryana. The provocation, however, was enough to snap a brittle alliance.

The next morning, 6 March, Chandra Shekhar called on President Venkataraman and submitted his resignation. He felt he had been pushed around enough by an increasingly aggressive Congress and a paranoid Rajiv who accused the prime minister of personally organizing the spying on him. Venkataraman was most displeased at the turn of events. As a former finance minister (1980–82), and that too the one who had negotiated a loan with the IMF in 1981, Venkataraman was aware of the nature and seriousness of the economic situation India was in.

He repeatedly cautioned Rajiv Gandhi not to destabilize Chandra Shekhar's government and, in his own words, 'was desperate to save the [Chandra Shekhar] ministry for at least another six months' to enable it to negotiate a loan with the IMF and restore stability to the balance of payments.

Rajiv was taken aback by Chandra Shekhar upping the ante. 'Rajiv wanted Chandra Shekhar to crawl, not resign', read the headline of an *Economic Times* news report filed by Seema Mustafa that week.

But Chandra Shekhar turned the tables on Rajiv by his unexpected move. Rajiv requested Maharashtra Congressman Sharad Pawar, a friend of Chandra Shekhar, to intervene on his behalf and get the prime minister to withdraw his resignation. Only two days earlier, on 4 March, Rajiv and Chandra Shekhar were in Baramati, Maharashtra, attending Pawar's daughter Supriya's wedding.

Pawar called on Chandra Shekhar and told him that there had been some misunderstanding. 'Congress doesn't want your government to fall. Please withdraw your resignation.'

An angry Chandra Shekhar shot back, 'Go back and tell him that Chandra Shekhar does not change his mind three times a day.'

If Prime Minister Chandra Shekhar was livid, his finance minister was worried. He had a deal with the IMF. If he presented a reform-oriented budget, the Fund would give India a lifeline that would avert a balance of payments crisis. Rajiv Gandhi had thrown a spanner in the works.

Accepting Chandra Shekhar's resignation, President Venkataraman dissolved the Lok Sabha and asked him to continue as caretaker prime minister until the new government was formed. Venkataraman notes in his autobiography that he felt 'sorry' to see Chandra Shekhar go.

Chapter 2

March: The Crisis

On 1 August 1990, Moody's, the New York-headquartered credit rating agency, placed India on 'credit watch for possible downgrading' because, as it explained, 'political conditions in India have weakened since our initial rating assignment [in 1987]'. Moody's decided to place India's ratings on review for a possible downgrade because it feared an increase in two kinds of risks. First, the risk of a short-term liquidity crunch leaving India unable to finance its external imbalance and forcing her to undertake a sharp balance of payments adjustment largely dependent on compressing domestic growth. In other words, curbing growth to curb imports in order to reduce the trade deficit. Second, the risk that measures selected to achieve the balance of payments adjustment in the short-term would disrupt the process of structural change, jeopardizing political support for efforts to improve India's international competitive position, in the medium term.

In 1987, Moody's had given India an A2/ Prime 1 investment grade rating. India had survived Indira Gandhi's assassination and Rajiv Gandhi's government seemed focused on economic modernization. In its assessment of the Indian economy at the time Moody's noted that: (*a*) India had a conservative tradition of keeping its external exposure within manageable limits; (*b*) that the government would maintain a steady pace in policy adjustment which would address such issues as the already high budget deficit and public enterprise inefficiency; and (*c*) it would undertake policy reform aimed at removing restraints on competition in the industrial sector.

At that time, Moody's also assumed that macroeconomic policy formulation and implementation in India would be coherent, consistent and timely, and that policy in the areas of most concern to the expansion of India's export-earning capacity would remain relatively immune from any turbulence in India's political arena.

In hindsight these seem brave, perhaps naïve, assumptions. It could also be asked if Western rating agencies were 'talking up' India at a time when other developing economies were in trouble, especially in Latin America and Africa, and global investors were looking for a good place to put their money in. This is no empty speculation. At least some people in the Ministry of Finance believed that Western rating agencies had boosted India's ratings in the second half of the 1980s, encouraging Indian borrowers to liberally borrow abroad and pile up external debt. Then, as if acting in tandem, they downgraded India in 1990, making an already precarious balance of payments situation worse.

Moody's reassessment of the India risk in August 1990 drew attention to the fiscal implications of the V. P. Singh government's decision to write off a part of the loan given by banks to farmers; the fiscal and economic impact of extending reservations; and the likelihood of a minority government taking adequate policy action to deal with growing external uncertainties. V. P. Singh's populism and 'a review of events since late 1987', as Moody's put it, had raised concerns about each of the three assumptions it had made in 1987. But it was not just a weakening of India's economic indicators that Moody's worried about. Its risk assessment report drew attention to increasing communal tension, continued tension in Punjab, Kashmir and the Northeast, and the situation in Tamil Nadu arising out of India's aborted involvement in the conflict in Sri Lanka.

Moody's returned in October 1990 to take another look at India and concluded that things had become worse. The rising external debt burden and falling foreign exchange reserves was a major worry. The rising fiscal deficit and decelerating government revenues was another. The Gulf crisis had raised fresh concerns about India's diminishing capacity to pay for its imports. Reviewing the economic, social and political situation in India, Moody's concluded that 'the government does not have the capacity to achieve a rapid improvement in the government budget deficit... and India's fractious domestic political conditions make it difficult to cut spending that sustains the government's political support.'

When the Chandra Shekhar government was formed in November 1990, it had a pretty good idea of how bad the economic situation was. Officials and economic advisers in government had fully briefed their political bosses. Blueprints had been prepared on what was to be done about fiscal, trade and industrial policy. But what India's political leaders had to come to terms with was that it was not just India's 'economic risk' that had gone up, so had its 'political risk'.

This was a new problem for India's economic managers. Independent India had faced balance of payments crises before and had dealt with a variety of other economic difficulties and crises in the near half century of its existence. However, during each such episode a government with a clear mandate and parliamentary majority was in office. For the first time in 1991 a minority government, bereft of any mandate, had been charged with the responsibility of dealing with an external payments crisis. For the first time, 'political risk' appeared on the radar of rating managers monitoring India.

On Thursday, 7 March 1991, Standard & Poor's, who had been a step behind Moody's till then, downgraded India's sovereign rating to BBB minus for long-term credit risk and to A3 for short-term credit risk, based on the conclusion that 'adverse economic conditions or changing circumstances are more likely to lead to a weakened capacity of the obligor to meet its financial commitments'. The 'obligor' in question was the government of the Republic of India. The 'changing circumstances' was a reference to political uncertainty and, as the rating agency saw it, the sharp upturn in political risk. A policy Lakshman rekha India had never crossed was of defaulting on its external payment obligations. That ignominy now stared India in the face.

■

The 1990-91 crisis was a long time in the making. Oxford economists Vijay Joshi and I. M. D. Little (Manmohan Singh's thesis supervisor at Oxford) date it all the way back to the 1970s, in a manner of speaking. At the end of a detailed professional analysis of political and economic developments from 1964 to 1991, and after noting many of the positive policy steps taken and their favourable impact on economic growth, Joshi and Little showed how the underlying macroeconomic situation was getting worse. All economic indicators pointed to trouble ahead. They concluded, 'Although the Economic Surveys [of the Finance

Ministry] made ritual references to these problems, there was no determined attempt to resolve them.'

Indira and Rajiv Gandhi were prime ministers for twenty-two of the twenty-seven years covered by Joshi and Little. From Nehru's time and through till the end of the 1970s, the Indian government had acquired a favourable reputation for its 'fiscal conservatism', thanks to what Joshi and Little term the 'Gladstonian fiscal outlook' of the Indian Civil Service, implying a commitment to 'sound finance' defined by balanced budgets. Even though the central government ran budget deficits during Nehru's and Indira's time, these were kept within manageable limits and many state governments ensured they had a revenue surplus. As populist pressures built up and political leaders began succumbing to them, budget and fiscal deficits mounted.

But things took a turn for the worse after 1980. As India's external debt kept rising, concerns began to be voiced about the country's external economic vulnerability. The current account deficit (CAD), that is the sum of the deficit in foreign trade and in capital flows as a share of national income, went up from -1.7 per cent of GDP in 1980–85 to -2.9 per cent in 1985–90. The total external debt trebled from US$20.6 billion in 1980–81 to US$64.4 billion in 1989–90, with the share of external debt in national income going up from 17.7 per cent to 24.5 per cent during that period. In all this, the share of private debt kept rising as the government liberalized external commercial borrowing and allowed Indian companies to borrow abroad. The key factor contributing to the sharp rise in CAD during the 1980s was a steep increase in imports—especially defence imports—and in external commercial borrowings of the private sector. After hovering below 3 per cent for a long time, the share of defence spending in national income went up to 3.6 per cent in 1986-87 and 1987-88, with most of this increased spending financing increased defence imports.

Political populism, on the other hand, contributed to increased government spending on subsidies. The share of fiscal deficit, that is the deficit in the government budget and the government's interest payment obligations in national income, shot up from an average of 6.3 per cent in the Sixth Plan period of 1980-85 to 8.2 per cent in the Seventh Plan period of 1985-90. Most economists regard this to be too high and prefer the number to be below 3 per cent. To make matters worse, the internal debt of the government also went up from 36 per cent of GDP at the end of 1980-81 to 54 per cent of GDP at the end of 1990-91. Interest payments by the government doubled during this decade, with their share in GDP going up from an annual average of 2.6 per cent in 1980-85 to 3.9 per cent in 1985-90.

Even with an overwhelming majority in Parliament, with over 400 MPs on the treasury benches in a house of 514 members, Rajiv Gandhi was unable to steer the economy away from fiscal mismanagement and crisis. Summing up their sharp indictment of the macroeconomic policies of the Rajiv Gandhi government, Joshi and Little concluded:

> The major mistake of macroeconomic policy lay in neglecting the danger signs evident in 1985-86 on the fiscal front. Fiscal deterioration was allowed to proceed apace. As a consequence, the current account deficit continued to worsen and domestic and foreign debt continued to increase at a dangerous rate. By the end of the decade, the macroeconomic fundamentals were out of joint. Even a

strictly temporary shock like the Gulf War was enough to trigger a full-scale crisis.

Placing greater emphasis on bad politics rather than just bad economics I. G. Patel remarked in a public lecture at the time:

> If the present crisis is the greatest we have faced since Independence, it is for no underlying economic factor which is more adverse now than what we have had to contend with in the past several decades. It is because successive governments in the 1980s chose to abdicate their responsibility to the nation for the sake of short-term partisan political gains and indeed out of sheer political cynicism.

Taking charge of a difficult situation, both Chandra Shekhar and Yashwant Sinha quickly put in place an economics team of high competence. Manmohan Singh was appointed adviser to the prime minister. He had just returned to India after a stint with the South Commission in Geneva before which he had been the central bank governor and deputy chairman of the Planning Commission. Finance Secretary S. Venkitaramanan, a highly regarded civil servant, was named governor, RBI. Yashwant Sinha got his own team into North Block with S. P. Shukla as finance secretary. With a new team still learning the ropes, the two who were till then minding the store, so to speak, Rangarajan and Nayyar, became the key actors and tasked to negotiate with the IMF.

Sinha took several measures to slow down the outflow of foreign exchange and reached out to several developed economies for help. India's traditional donors were requested to speed up the transfer of aid funds. However, the message from most of them was simple—tap the IMF, secure its imprimatur at which point we can step in and help. India's foreign exchange reserves had plummeted since August 1990 and Moody's and the Japanese Bond Research Institute (JBRI) had already downgraded India's sovereign credit rating.

In December 1990 Finance Minister Sinha recalls he had two 'immediate priorities'. 'First, to secure whatever assistance we could from the IMF on an emergency basis and, second, to prepare a path-breaking budget that would address the accumulated problems of the Indian economy.'

■

As we have seen, by mid-February 1991, Rajiv Gandhi, nervous at the progress made by the Chandra Shekhar government, forced a delay in the budget presentation. And, even before this important budgetary business could be concluded, the partnership between Chandra Shekhar and Rajiv Gandhi came apart. On 6 March, Chandra Shekhar submitted his resignation.

President Venkataraman had only one thing on his mind. He did not want a political impasse to create a financial and administrative crisis. If the Parliament did not vote in time to approve government spending for the ensuing financial year, then the entire government would come to a halt on 1 April, the beginning of the new financial year. Venkataraman was prescient enough to hold on to that letter of resignation and accepted it only on 7 March after he made sure that the Lok Sabha had voted to allow government spending to continue.

The inability of the government to present a regular budget resulted in a further downgrading of India's sovereign credit rating. The problem was no longer one of numbers—fiscal deficit, external debt and such like. What was till then an economic crisis, made worse by the Gulf War and the spike in oil prices, became a crisis of confidence. India's ability to manage a crisis was now in doubt. As the Finance Ministry's *Economic Survey* of 1991–92 summed up: 'The payments crisis of 1990–91 was not, however, due simply to a deterioration in the trade account; it was accompanied by other adverse developments on the capital account reflecting the loss of confidence in the government's ability to manage the situation.'

Something drastic had to be done to shore up the reserves and the first act of desperation was to 'bring the shutters down' on imports, as the then chief economic adviser Deepak Nayyar described the government's decision of 20 March to impose draconian physical controls on imports. Whatever was needed to be done to avoid a default would be done. The prime minister had no doubt that this needed to be done.

In a hard-hitting editorial comment the next day, titled 'Sledgehammer blow', the *Economic Times* (21 March 1991) was extremely critical of the political leadership for allowing things to come to this pass. 'With a caretaker government in office, the Finance Ministry was left with no option other than abandoning its earlier attempt to seek further support from the IMF. These developments have had the combined effect of heightening the concern among India's creditors about its political and economic prospects in the short run.'

But this was not enough. Squeezing imports reduced foreign exchange spending on the trade account. It was a solution on the demand side. But with dollars flying out of foreign currency accounts thanks to non-resident Indians losing confidence, the government had to get a grip on the capital account as well. A supply side solution was needed. The simplest, though politically tough, option available was to convert India's gold stocks into hard cash. A proposal to this effect had been examined in detail by the RBI as early as December 1990. It was revived in March 1991, the decision was taken in April and executed in May.

When Cabinet Secretary Chandra briefed Prime Minister Chandra Shekhar on the RBI's recommendation, his initial reaction was one of disbelief and anger.

'I do not want to go down in history as the man who sold gold for buying oil,' said a furious Chandra Shekhar.

'But, sir,' replied Chandra, 'you have to choose between going down in history as the prime minister who mortgaged gold or as the prime minister who defaulted.'

For most Indians gold has sentimental value. A family that mortgages its gold to finance its daily needs is a family in despair. Revealing to the nation that the government had mortgaged gold was, therefore, a particularly difficult political decision. Aware of this political hesitation on the prime minister's part, a highly placed economic policymaker recommended default. Other developing countries had done so. Why not India?

Both Chandra and Nayyar had to explain to the prime minister the consequences of a default. To begin with, the rupee would take a serious knock. There could be a run on major banks. External trade, including vital imports like oil and food, could freeze. India's global standing would be seriously compromised. India's hard-earned reputation for reasonably sound macroeconomic management would simply evaporate. Foreign creditors and governments would acquire enormous influence over Indian policy. Many other developing countries had lived through that disempowering experience when a sovereign nation becomes subservient to the whims of bankers and their masters.

Chandra Shekhar had to bite the bullet, so to speak. If Lal Bahadur Shastri has entered the history books, despite his brief tenure, it is because of the way he handled the 1965 war with Pakistan; Chandra Shekhar too would have found his place in history despite the brevity of his tenure if he had had the opportunity to act. But he didn't. Never before had India's politics become so dysfunctional. Never before had an economic crisis, compounded by geopolitical events far away, lowered global confidence in India to the extent that it had in March 1991. The prime minister authorized the mortgaging of gold to avoid default.

Twenty metric tonnes of confiscated gold, worth US$200 million, held in its vaults was made available by the RBI to the State Bank of India for sale, with a repurchase option, to the Union Bank of Switzerland. This was the first time India was selling gold to avoid default and to ensure that its external payment obligations were met.

Both the Bank of England and the Bank of Japan demanded the actual shipment of gold to their vaults. It would not just be a paper settlement. Gold bars of acceptable quality had to be airlifted and sent out. Though the final shipments began only in July, after the Narasimha Rao government took charge, the groundwork had to be done in secrecy through the summer months. RBI governor Venkitaraman and deputy governor Rangarajan personally supervised the entire operation.

Chapter 3

May: The Elections

Rajiv Gandhi was assassinated at Sriperumbudur near Chennai on 21 May 1991. On 20 May, the first phase of polling in the general elections had been conducted. The next day Rajiv set out to campaign for the second phase and arrived in Tamil Nadu. At a public rally a young woman walked up to him and pulled the trigger on the suicide vest she was wearing. Rajiv Gandhi and at least fourteen others were killed and many more injured. With his death the long democratic reign of the Nehru-Gandhis ended.

Jawaharlal Nehru was prime minister of free India from August 1947 till his death in May 1964. His daughter Indira Gandhi served two tenures as prime minister—from January 1966 to March 1977 and from January 1980 to October 1984, when she was assassinated. On her death her son Rajiv Gandhi, an airline pilot-turned-party functionary, was immediately sworn in as prime minister and was elected in his own right, riding a political sympathy wave generated by his mother's assassination, in December 1984. He served a full term till December 1989, when his party was defeated in the elections.

Three generations of the Nehru–Gandhi family had ruled India for thirty-seven of the first forty-two years after Independence. Coalition and minority governments have been the rule since 1991, till Narendra Modi led the BJP to victory in May 2014, establishing a single party majority government for the first time since 1989.

On 22 May 1991, the Congress Working Committee (CWC) met and invited Rajiv's widow, the Italian-born Sonia Gandhi, to take charge as Congress president. When this invitation was conveyed to Sonia, she declined the offer stating, according to Fotedar, that 'she was not interested in active politics'.

India's oldest political party, the vanguard of the country's struggle for freedom, the party that at one time governed every single state in this vast subcontinent, had become feudal in its instincts. When Indira Gandhi died, her son Rajiv was made party president and prime minister. Senior party leaders, like Pranab Mukherjee, who may have even fleetingly wondered whether someone more senior in the party and government ought to step in, even as an interim prime minister, received their comeuppance.

Mukherjee, now President of India, vehemently denies in his autobiography that he had any such ambitions. He dismisses as 'false and spiteful' reports to the effect that he had hoped to be invited to head the government after Indira Gandhi's assassination in 1984. But why should such hopes be regarded as sinful? In no democracy would anyone regard speculation about a senior party member nursing such ambition as 'spiteful'. However, in the feudal milieu of the Indira Congress such whispers could prove to be politically fatal.

In his defence, Mukherjee quotes P. C. Alexander who wrote in his autobiography: 'A group of individuals, with malicious intent, later spread a canard that Pranab Mukherjee had staked his claim to be sworn in as interim PM and had to be persuaded with great difficulty to withdraw his claim.' It would seem Rajiv believed those who spread the canard. On being elected back to power in December 1984, Rajiv chose not to induct Mukherjee into his council of ministers.

Recalls Mukherjee, 'When I learnt of my ouster from the cabinet, I was shell-shocked and flabbergasted. I could not believe it. But I composed myself, and sat alongside my wife as she watched the swearing-in ceremony on television.' In April 1986, Mukherjee was expelled from the Congress, only to be rehabilitated in 1988. For three full years, between January 1985 and February 1988 when Mukherjee was rehabilitated, Rajiv and Mukherjee did not meet even once.

After Rajiv's assassination, Mukherjee may have wondered about the possibility of becoming the prime minister once again. However, recalling the day Sonia declined the party presidentship and the party chose PV, Mukherjee does not betray any bitterness and writes: 'To the dismay of the CWC members Soniaji… maintained a stoic silence throughout this period [of mourning]… Following Soniaji's refusal [to become party president], it was decided that P. V. Narasimha Rao, the senior-most member of the CWC (part of the committee since 1976) and Chairman of the Central Election Coordination Committee, would be invited to assume presidentship of the party.'

It was one thing to elect Rajiv as Indira's successor, for he was already in active politics and had taken charge as the party leader, and it was quite another to elect to that position the foreign-born widow of a slain leader, who till that day had virtually had no involvement in politics and party affairs. Moreover, the party leadership in 1984 consisted mainly of people whose political career was made by loyalty to Indira after the Emergency. Arjun Singh, A. K. Antony, Pranab Mukherjee, PV and many more became senior union ministers only after Indira's return to power in 1980. They may have legitimately felt they owed it to Indira to elect her son as their new leader.

In 1991, few in that CWC owed much to Rajiv. He had squandered the verdict of 1984, presided over the party's defeat in 1989, done little to strengthen the party during 1989-91. Yet, when he died, an entire generation of Congress leaders who had made their individual political careers across the length and breadth of a vast subcontinent of a republican democracy seemed to morph into medieval courtiers, hailing, 'The King is Dead! Long Live the Queen!' Perhaps they felt they didn't have an option because most of them owed at least part of their success to their unwavering allegiance to the family that had seized control of the Delhi durbar.

The consequent division in party leadership—between those who believed the Congress ought to have a future independent of the Nehru-Gandhi family and those who could not imagine such a future—has remained a fissure within ever since.

The second and subsequent phases of polling were postponed and held in June. When results were out in mid-June, no political party had a clear majority, but the Congress emerged as the single largest party in the Lok Sabha.

While seniority in the CWC helped PV become party president, the question to be resolved was whether he would also become the prime minister. During Nehru's time—and even during Indira's first tenure as prime minister, till 1977—the prime minister only occasionally became party president. More often than not the two posts were held by different individuals. But, after

1978, Indira Gandhi held both posts and Rajiv continued that system. In most democracies majority support within the party is a necessary qualification for heading the party's government when the party wins an election. In the Congress system developed under Indira and her son, control over government, its machinery and its munificence, became the route to acquire and retain dominance within the party.

Would PV remain content with just the party presidentship or would he expect to also be prime minister? Several names of prospective prime ministerial candidates popped up in the media. Arjun Singh was mentioned as being popular among north Indians in the Congress. Sharad Pawar, at the time the chief minister of Maharashtra, signalled his interest. Those close to Rajiv looked to Sonia for guidance. Surely, the elected MPs would have to have a role too? Would they remain mute spectators allowing power brokers and a coterie around Sonia to pick and choose the prime minister? Would they now demand that their voice be heard? Whom would they favour? I decided to meet PV to find out what was happening.

■

It was the middle of June 1991. Delhi was simmering. As results of the elections to the Lok Sabha rolled out, it was clear that the Congress would fall short of a majority but would be the single largest party. On 17 June, the *Times of India* carried a front-page news report quoting Maharashtra Chief Minister Sharad Pawar as saying that MPs from his state would play a 'key role' in deciding who would be prime minister.

'Though Mr Pawar evaded questions', said the news report filed by an unnamed Special Correspondent, 'it was obvious that he is very much in the race for the Prime Minister's job.'

The next day, on 18 June, the *Times of India*'s Mumbai city bureau chief, Rajdeep Sardesai, filed a report headlined, 'Pawar sets sights on Delhi'.

I wondered if a Maratha would finally succeed in occupying the seat of power at the Delhi durbar. At the height of its reign, the Maratha empire under the Peshwas of Pune did envelop Delhi, the seat of Mughal power, but, curiously, the Mughal residents in Delhi's fort were left alone. The Peshwas remained in Pune. Even though the Marathas had vanquished the Mughals, no Maratha king ever sat on the throne in Delhi.

The first Maratha leader to occupy a position of power in democratic India was Yashwantrao Balwantrao Chavan. The chief minister of Maharashtra in 1960-62, Chavan was always viewed as a potential prime minister. He began his career in national politics as defence minister in Jawaharlal Nehru's cabinet immediately after the 1962 debacle. Chinese troops had crushed their ill-equipped and unprepared Indian counterparts along the disputed border between the two Asian giants in the high Himalayas. Chavan restored military morale and ensured adequate investments were finally made in defence. Of prime ministerial calibre, Chavan was widely viewed as one of the most capable members of Indira Gandhi's cabinet. But he never made it to the top job. Sharad Pawar was his protégé and regarded Chavan his mentor and inspiration. Would the protégé now make history?

On 20 June, I dropped in at 9 Motilal Nehru Marg, the Lutyens's Delhi bungalow of P. V. Narasimha Rao, hoping to find out what was happening. There was not a soul in sight as I drove my Fiat car into PV's compound. PV's personal secretary, Ram Khandekar, welcomed me as I alighted and walked into the house. On entering PV's living room I found him seated, attired in his usual white cotton lungi and vest, chatting with fellow Congressman Bhagwat Jha Azad—a former chief minister of Bihar and father of cricket player Kirti Azad. I did my usual namaskaram. I was invited to sit down and offered a cup of tea. I asked PV what he thought of all the news reports in the *Times of India* about Sharad Pawar becoming prime minister.

'It is a Bombay newspaper,' said PV, nonchalantly. The metropolis was not yet called Mumbai and the TOI was at that time viewed as a Bombay daily. New Delhi's leader was the *Hindustan Times*.

'The editor [Dilip Padgaonkar] is Maharashtrian. Their political bureau chief [Subhash Kirpekar] is a Maharashtrian. All the reports are coming from Bombay. What else will they say?'

Azad laughed. I did too. PV chuckled. I had my answer.

PV was a man of few words. Known for his refusal to respond to queries and demands for instructions from colleagues and subordinates (and his pout), PV became famous for the statement attributed to him: 'Not taking a decision is also a decision'. For a man who knew a dozen languages (he could fluently read, write and speak over half a dozen) and was known to have had a series of romantic entanglements, he was surprisingly uncommunicative in person.

Though we were both from Hyderabad, my association with PV was fleeting till I moved to Delhi in 1990. After a decade of teaching economics at the Central University of Hyderabad, I switched to journalism and joined the editorial team at the *Economic Times* in New Delhi in July 1990. I called on PV a few times after that. He was, in those months, preparing to move back to Hyderabad. His close aide, P. V. R. K. Prasad, a relative of mine and PV's secretary when the latter was chief minister of Andhra Pradesh, would later tell me that PV was contemplating becoming a priest at the Courtallam Peetham. He had also planned to associate himself with the activities of the Bharatiya Vidya Bhavan's Rajaji Institute and the Swami Ramananda Tirtha Rural Institute. In this connection he had been back in touch with my father, whom he had known from the day he became a member of the Andhra Pradesh state legislature in 1957. My father was then Collector of Karimnagar, the district in which PV's Manthani constituency was located.

In 1959, PV had enrolled for a training programme in community development at the Development Officers' Training Centre, newly set up by the Union Community Development Ministry near Hyderabad. My father was its principal. He and PV would spend the evening walking around the campus, discussing economics, politics, books and writers and a range of national issues. Over the years the two developed a close bond. PV would often confide in him some of his most private thoughts.

In September 1971, PV was named chief minister of Andhra Pradesh as part of a deal to end an agitation for the bifurcation of the state and the creation of Telangana. Kasu Brahmananda Reddy from coastal Andhra, a Congress Party supremo in the state, had to step down as chief minister. While the agitation for a separate Telangana state was led by Chenna Reddy, also a Congressman who later formed the Telangana Praja Samiti, Indira Gandhi chose to name PV as chief minister rather than Chenna Reddy. He was viewed as a safe bet, a Brahmin without a political base in a state whose politics was dominated, at the time, by the Reddys, an economically well-off and politically powerful land-owning caste.

As chief minister, PV pushed the implementation of land

reforms, aimed partly at weakening the political base of the Reddy and Velama landlord communities in the Telangana region. An alliance of Backward Castes, Dalits, Muslims and Brahmins supported PV. But the coastal Andhra politicians, especially the Reddys and Kammas, proved smarter. They launched an agitation for the creation of a separate Andhra state and PV's inability to deal with that situation resulted in the central government imposing President's Rule in January 1973. PV then moved to New Delhi and was made a party general secretary.

As a student at the Jawaharlal Nehru University, in 1974–76, I would often run into PV in the home of the political science professor, Rasheeduddin Khan. Khan was at the time also a member of the Rajya Sabha and PV knew him well. At this time PV also frequented the JNU library and seminars on campus. In January 1975 I had gone with friends to watch the Republic Day parade. We arrived at Rajpath early enough to secure chairs for ourselves. Late to arrive, PV had no chair to sit on. I went up to him and invited him to take my chair. It was an embarrassing situation for both of us. He was, after all, a former chief minister. No one around us had recognized him.

PV remained loyal to Indira Gandhi through the Emergency years and after. He took this time to educate himself in national and international affairs. His skills as a writer were recognized when he was called upon to write party manifestos and political resolutions. On her return to power in 1980, Indira Gandhi rewarded him with the external affairs portfolio. During the 1980s he headed all the top ministries on Raisina Hill, where the South and North Blocks are located, barring finance.

PV was regarded as a good and effective external affairs minister, though his tenure as home minister was marred by the government's inept handling of the anti-Sikh riots following Indira's assassination. After Indira's death, Rajiv Gandhi retained PV in his council of ministers, assigning him the Defence Ministry and then the newly-created human resource development portfolio. He was later made external affairs minister. However, Rajiv rarely sought his advice on political matters. A new generation of Rajiv's buddies and family cronies were now running the show. To be fair to Rajiv, there would have been a generation gap separating him from PV. This would have been made worse by the upper-class prejudices of his globalized Doon School friends. Rajiv lived in a world where everyone around him ate with forks and knives. PV was more comfortable eating with his fingers.

In his absorbing account of PV's reform initiatives, Gurcharan Das laments that PV was never as revolutionary as Deng Xiaoping. But there was at least one thing in common between Deng and PV. Both had been banished by their boss. Deng was sent into political oblivion by Mao Zedong for decades. Rao was sidelined by Rajiv for a few years. Deng returned to Beijing to overturn Mao's world. PV returned to government to complete what Rajiv was clearly politically ill-equipped to pursue. When Rajiv went to Beijing in 1988 and had his famous meeting with Deng Xiaoping, PV, then external affairs minister, was kept out of all meetings. Ironically, it is PV who later came to be viewed as India's Deng!

PV had been elected to the Lok Sabha in 1984 and 1989 from Ramtek in Maharashtra. But he was denied a ticket in the 1991 elections. Realizing that Rajiv had intended to sideline him as he had Pranab Mukherjee, PV planned to go into political retirement. However, while Mukherjee had to quit the Congress Party (and was later rehabilitated), PV was merely denied an election ticket. Ironically, when Rajiv Gandhi was assassinated, PV chaired the CWC meeting that condoled his death.

If Rajiv and PV lived in different worlds, Sonia and PV came from different planets. There was never any real social connect between the two. So PV could not have relied on getting her support. Instead he had to rely on the goodwill of elected Congress MPs, especially those from the south.

■

The fact that PV was sitting at home on the morning of 20 June with just one friend, a relatively unimportant party leader, paints a somewhat misleading picture. We now know from the memoirs of Natwar Singh, Sharad Pawar, Fotedar and the late P. C. Alexander that much was going on in political and party circles in Delhi. PV's friends and supporters were active, lobbying politicians and business leaders. Knowing his rival Pawar was close to Mumbai's business leaders, PV's friends reached out to them, seeking their support or at least assurance of their political neutrality.

By end of day on 20 June, the Congress Parliamentary Party (CPP) elected PV leader. President Venkataraman then established an important parliamentary convention by deciding that he would invite the leader of the single largest group in the Lok Sabha to form a government and secure parliamentary approval within a month. Venkataraman was keen to ensure political stability at a time of economic crisis. He floated the idea of a 'national government' that would have the support of most, if not all, political parties. There were no takers for this idea. He then opted to invite PV but spoke informally to opposition leaders to ensure that the new government would not be voted out till it had pulled the economy out of crisis. At 7.30 p.m., on 20 June 1991, PV met the president and was invited to form the government. On 21 June, exactly a week before his seventieth birthday, he was sworn in as prime minister.

Most recent memoirs of that time suggest that PV scored over Pawar and other aspirants like Arjun Singh, because Sonia Gandhi and the 'family loyalists' backed him. The behaviour of the coterie and the Congress leadership at the time seemed predicated on the premise that Rajiv Gandhi was destined to return to power as his mother did in 1980. They assumed India's prime ministership was there for Rajiv's taking; that, upon his death, it was for the heirs of Rajiv to decide who would be India's next prime minister. Perhaps they assumed PV would be more biddable than any of the others. That he would be a loyal yes man, a mere rubber stamp, who would do as he was told because he was very old and a political non-entity. However, this remains a simplistic explanation. What is plausible is the theory that Sonia loyalists had few credible options apart from PV. According to Natwar Singh, Sonia was willing to back Shankar Dayal Sharma for the post, but he turned down the offer on account of poor health. Sharma was India's vice-president at the time and had an entire year to go. He may well have preferred the guarantee of another year in that job to the uncertainty of heading a minority government. Sharma would have also assumed that he would be in line for presidentship in a year's time. Five assured years as head of state seemed more reassuring than the uncertainty of heading a minority government.

■

Historians do not fancy counterfactuals. Economists, on the other hand, like to debate 'what if'. Political scientists tend to be agnostic on the issue. Surprisingly few political analysts have asked the obvious counterfactual about 1991. What if Rajiv Gandhi had not been assassinated? Would the Indira Congress have been voted back to office? If the Congress had failed to get a clear majority, would Rajiv still have headed a Congress-led coalition?

The simple answer to those questions is: unlikely. Consider the facts.

In 1989 Rajiv Gandhi led his party to ignominious defeat. The Indira Congress's vote share had gone down to 39.5 per cent from 49.1 per cent in 1984. The number of Congress candidates elected to the Lok Sabha went down even more precipitously from 404 in 1984 to 197 in 1989. This resounding defeat did not cost him the leadership of his party as one would normally expect in democratic politics.

For one thing, those who had already challenged Rajiv's leadership, led by former colleague V. P. Singh, had left the parent party to form the Janata Dal. As for those who chose to stay within, loyalty to the Nehru-Gandhi family became the cheapest ticket to political relevance. The coterie of loyalists, ranging from those whose political career was made by Jawaharlal Nehru and Indira Gandhi, to those who entered the party as friends and followers of Rajiv or Sanjay, ensured that Rajiv remained the party boss.

Indira Gandhi's populist political platform, her international reputation as a strong woman leader, and her assassination had created such an aura around her that many Congress leaders were happy to even refer to their party as 'Indira Congress'. Rajiv was the beneficiary of his mother's personality cult and there were enough of his acolytes within the party to foster his personal brand. But all that was of no use when popular support slipped away and rival political platforms gained ascendance.

The coterie would not give up so easily. When an internal coup in the Janata Dal forced Prime Minister V. P. Singh to quit office in November 1990, an attempt was made to re-install Rajiv as a minority prime minister. Family loyalist Fotedar claims he made the case to President Venkataraman. With 197 MPs in the Lok Sabha, Rajiv was the leader of the largest party in Parliament, Fotedar reminded the President. The Janata Dal had only 143 MPs, but had formed the government with the support of the Communist and other regional parties. Since that coalition had come apart, the leader of the single largest party should be asked to try and form a government. Venkataraman did not bite.

The Congress, the president presumably calculated, would need the backing of seventy-five more MPs and he wasn't convinced that Rajiv could muster the required support. As has been mentioned, according to Fotedar, Venkataraman was willing to swear in Pranab Mukherjee as prime minister. Clearly, he felt Mukherjee would be able to win over the required number.

Mukherjee himself has a very different recollection of what transpired at the time. 'The President sought Rajiv's views on the situation,' recalls Mukherjee. 'He then asked if, as the largest party, the Congress was willing to form the government. But the Congress once again declined. Rajiv indicated that the Congress would extend unconditional support to Chandra Shekhar if he formed the government.'

If Fotedar was right, why then did Rajiv Gandhi extend his party's support to Chandra Shekhar rather than risk Mukherjee's elevation to prime minister? Circumstantial evidence suggests that Rajiv had intended to bring the government down at a time suitable to him so that he could return to the voters and seek another mandate to rule. Sharad Pawar, at the time chief minister of Maharashtra, concurs with this view: 'Rajiv had propped up the Chandra Shekhar government merely as an ad hoc arrangement. Rajiv was only buying time so that the Congress could gear up for the next general elections.'

Perhaps Rajiv felt that had he allowed a Congress-led government to be formed with Mukherjee at the helm, the party, the government and the game could very well have slipped out of his hand. The Chandra Shekhar government fell earlier than Rajiv had planned. It was not on account of Rajiv's political initiative that Chandra Shekhar had quit, but because the latter was no longer willing to remain a prime minister at Rajiv's beck and call. Unlike V. P. Singh, who was a junior colleague of Rajiv's before turning against him, Chandra Shekhar was a Congressman of the 1960s. He was angry about being pushed around by a political Johnny-come-lately and his coterie. Whatever the reasons, the Chandra Shekhar government was terminated. Elections were called.

Had Congress secured a clear majority in the Lok Sabha in the elections that followed, the president would have had to invite Rajiv to form the government. But the question that is moot is would the Congress have had the numbers?

That's the key counterfactual of 1991. An *India Today* opinion poll conducted on 20 May, a day before Rajiv's assassination, forecast only 190 seats for the Congress in the ongoing elections. The 1991 Lok Sabha elections were to be held in several phases. When Rajiv was killed on the second day of voting, other phases were postponed and subsequently held on 12 and 15 June.

Electoral data clearly shows a 9 percentage point swing in votes in favour of the Congress in the post-assassination phase. This 'sympathy wave' in favour of the Congress has been analysed by psephologists who make three points: First, that if voting on 20 May (in Andhra Pradesh, Bihar, Haryana, Himachal Pradesh, Madhya Pradesh, Rajasthan, Sikkim, Uttar Pradesh, West Bengal, Andaman and Nicobar Islands, Chandigarh, Delhi, and Lakshadweep) was adequately representative of the national mood and subsequent voting followed the same pattern, then the Congress would not have secured anything close to a majority of seats.

Second, the swing in favour of the Congress after 20 May was mainly on account of a sharp rise in the votes cast by women, Muslims, Scheduled Castes and Backward Classes—the traditional support base of the Indira Congress. This fact suggests that traditional Congress voters had not felt enthused enough to come out in large numbers and vote for Rajiv Gandhi on the first phase of polling. It is only after his assassination that they ventured out and voted in large numbers in favour of the Congress. The sympathy wave was also more pronounced in peninsular India than in the Gangetic Plain.

The data also shows that the main losers in this switch between the pre- and post-assassination phases of polling were the BJP, the CPI (M) and the Telugu Desam Party (TDP), all of which had done well in the pre-assassination phase and saw a sharp dip in their vote shares after 21 May. While the Congress won 50 of the 196 seats for which polling was held on 20 May (a success rate of 25.51 per cent), it won 177 of 285 seats for which polling was held in June 1991 (a success rate of 62.11 per cent).

Now, suppose the final result in June 1991 was such that the Congress had 190 seats, as the *India Today* poll data suggested it would, the BJP had 140, the Communists had 45, Janata Dal had 75 and the assortment of regional parties had about 60—all in the realm of possibility given the voting trends recorded. Who would have been able to form the government? The Communists and the Janata Dal, with their 120 MPs, may have preferred the Congress over the BJP, but would they have agreed to Rajiv heading that government? The post-2004 bonhomie between Sonia and the Communist parties was not the state of affairs that existed with Rajiv. The Communist parties supported V. P. Singh's government in 1989 and opposed Rajiv's economic policy initiatives.

Would the Communists and Janata Dal have supported a Congress-led government albeit with a more acceptable Congressman as prime minister? If so, would it have been Mukherjee or PV or someone else? If that coalition was led by the Congress, would President Venkataraman have been able to persuade Rajiv to name Mukherjee as its head, or would PV have been Rajiv's choice?

The purpose of this counterfactual thought experiment is to make the point that by the summer of 1991 the Congress Party was already grappling with the consequences of the decline of the dynasty. It was only natural that senior Congress leaders like Venkataraman, Mukherjee and PV were thinking about their party's future beyond the Nehru-Gandhis. Could someone other than Rajiv Gandhi head a Congress-led coalition?

■

If, in 1991, the Congress had managed to win no more seats than it had in 1989, how would that have impacted the party and Rajiv's standing in it? If the BJP had done better and had secured more than the 119 seats that it finally did, who would have been its allies? Could the Third Front of 1996-98 been formed in 1991? Who would have been its prime minister?

Consider the facts again. We know from Pranab Mukherjee's

autobiography that there was no love lost between him and Rajiv. As we know, Rajiv had expelled Mukherjee from the Congress Party in 1986. He returned from political exile to rejoin the Congress in 1988, but was not given any important responsibilities. At the time of the 1989 elections the Congress Party's manifesto was in fact drafted by PV, and it was PV who sought to rehabilitate Mukherjee by seeking his help in its drafting.

Finally, between 1980 and 1989, PV had held four of the five most important portfolios in the union government—home, defence, external affairs and human resource development. Mukherjee had only been finance minister and that too for three years from January 1982 to December 1984.

So the upshot of it all is that even if Rajiv Gandhi had not been killed in May 1991, the Congress could have at best formed a coalition government. Such a coalition, like all coalitions, would have required a compromise candidate as its head. The odds are that PV would have been the Congress prime minister despite not even being given a party ticket to contest the elections. Apart from the fact that he was considered a family 'loyalist' by the Nehru-Gandhis, he had other qualifications. He was not a Brahmin from UP and so wouldn't undermine the political base of the Nehru-Gandhis. But he would be acceptable to UP's upper-caste politicians, given his caste and language credentials.

Interestingly, there are now several theories about how PV became prime minister. As mentioned earlier, while Natwar Singh's view is that Shankar Dayal Sharma was Sonia's choice, Fotedar does not even mention this possibility. He suggests that Sonia had to choose between PV, Pawar and Arjun Singh and that it was her decision to back PV that clinched the deal.

Pawar has a slightly different recollection of events. While he admits that PV emerged as a consensus choice after efforts were made to 'gauge the mood' of elected MPs, he credits Sonia Gandhi with tilting the scale in PV's favour 'because he was old and was not in good shape'. Pawar thinks PV had an edge over him by as many as 35 MPs. This, however, is an underestimation. Pawar was assured of the support of only the 38 MPs from Maharashtra, while PV had the support of all the 89 MPs from the south. He would, after all, be the first south Indian to head a government in Delhi.

Mukherjee, widely credited with a very good memory, has a more precise recollection of events: 'An elaborate consensus-building effort was initiated and MPs were summoned one by one to ascertain their views. K. Karunakaran was nominated by PV and Siddhartha Shankar Ray by Sharad Pawar to hear out the MPs' opinion. It finally became clear that the majority of the MPs wanted PV, who had served as a senior minister in the Cabinets of both Indira Gandhi and Rajiv Gandhi. PV was also helped by the backing of eighty-five MPs from the southern states of Andhra Pradesh, Karnataka, Kerala and Tamil Nadu.' The exact number was 89, including Pondicherry and the island territories.

Numbers matter. Consider the composition of the CPP. Of the 227 elected MPs, as many as 142 hailed from peninsular India. Only 43 hailed from the four major Hindi-speaking states—Bihar, MP, UP and Rajasthan. This weakened the case for a north Indian candidate. Shankar Dayal Sharma may have been wise enough to understand this, though he and Arjun Singh hailed from MP, which had the largest contingent of 27 from among the Hindi-speaking states. Pawar's ambition was stoked by the fact that Maharashtra had elected the single largest contingent of 38 MPs.

In his biography of PV, Sitapati has suggested that PV may

have shied away from a direct contest with Pawar by rejecting Pawar's demand for a secret ballot. This is an over-reading of events. The fact is that the Congress high command has always adopted one-on-one confidential consultations with elected MLAs as a way of picking winners for the post of chief minister in the states. This was the first time since Morarji's challenge of Indira that the party had to choose between rival contenders for the prime minister's job. It adopted the same procedure of confidential consultations in lieu of secret ballot.

PV reached out to Pawar, convincing him that at fifty-one the Maharashtrian strongman was twenty years younger and had a long political career ahead of him. PV was not only hitting seventy, he was not in good shape and so could assure Pawar that time was on the latter's side. P. C. Alexander played a role, according to Pawar, by acting as an intermediary. Both PV and Pawar trusted Alexander and so the latter was able to facilitate an accord between the Telangana and the Maratha politicians. There are those who suggest that some influential business leaders also opted to back PV over Pawar.

Few analysts are willing to recognize that by 1990 the north-south divide within the Congress had become quite acute. This regional divide within the party came to the fore when the southern states remained loyal to Indira Gandhi even after the Emergency. In recognition of this fact, Indira contested from Karnataka in 1978 and Andhra Pradesh in 1980.

Neither Nehru nor Indira allowed this regional sentiment to overwhelm the party. Rajiv Gandhi, on the other hand, surrounded himself with political advisers and civil servants from the north. This despite the fact that the south voted massively for the Congress in 1984. The few south Indian leaders Rajiv had around him were either rootless politicians, like P. Shiv Shankar, or those disliked in their own home states. His arrogant and rude treatment of Andhra Pradesh Chief Minister T. Anjaiah, whom he publicly reprimanded on the tarmac at Hyderabad's Begumpet airport for some lapse, had a catastrophic impact on the fortunes of the Congress in that state. Telugu film actor N. T. Rama Rao's TDP greatly benefited from its campaign against Rajiv for hurting Telugu pride and sentiment.

PV counted on this southern sentiment and the southern MPs remained loyal to him. The problem of Maharashtra dissipated when Pawar was named defence minister. In bringing Pawar and S. B. Chavan into defence and home respectively, and Madhavsinh Solanki into external affairs, PV gave peninsular India its due. East India too went with PV.

In short, PV was not 'nominated' as prime minister by Sonia Gandhi and her coterie. They may have tilted the scales in his favour, but that is also because they would have recognized that a large majority of MPs, almost a 100 out of the 227, hailing from the southern states, would have preferred PV over Shankar Dayal Sharma, Arjun Singh and even Sharad Pawar.

■

The manner of PV's elevation to the nation's top job gave the Congress renewed hope in its future. Nehru's daughter and grandson had been killed. The question of 'After Nehru Who?' had unnerved the party in the early 1960s. That of 'After the Nehru-Gandhis Who?' could have been far more debilitating. Rajiv's children were too young. His widow was European, howsoever loyal the family's retainers remained. If the right choice had not been made, the party could have disintegrated.

The Nehru-Gandhi family retainers and cronies, the nondescript men and women who acquired power and wealth doing the family's bidding, were in fact doing a disservice to the Congress by repeatedly emphasizing the primacy of the family in the party. This was the way smaller, regional, sectarian and caste-based parties were run, with political power passing from one generation to the next. The Congress owed it to the nation to renew its democratic character as a modern political party. PV and his generation joined the Congress because it was an organizational expression of the patriotic and democratic sentiments of the Indian people. They did not join the Congress because they liked any one individual—Gandhi or Nehru or Bose or Patel. The Congress was a movement, and became a political party. In their twilight years, however, that generation saw the Congress turn into a family enterprise.

PV's election as party leader showed that the Congress could still draw on its own resources and find an ordinary Congressman tall enough to become prime minister. There could still be life beyond a single family for India's oldest political party. Younger leaders like Pawar, Arjun Singh, Madhavrao Scindia and many more could imagine, without being expelled from the party, that if PV could be prime minister, maybe they could aspire to succeed him. That is how normal political parties renew themselves—by giving hope to younger leaders. 1991 was that moment of hope for the Congress.

Conscious of this wellspring of democratic sentiment and aspiration within his party, PV called for organizational elections in the run-up to an AICC session where ordinary party members would vote and decide the composition of the party's highest decision-making body—the Congress Working Committee. We will examine that a little later.

It took PV a full two years to secure a majority in Parliament. In July 1993 his government won a vote of confidence in Parliament and further consolidated its position. This enabled him to complete his full term in office. No other prime minister from outside the Nehru-Gandhi family had done so until then. Not Morarji Desai from Gujarat, not Charan Singh or V. P. Singh from UP, not Chandra Shekhar from Bihar. As I have mentioned earlier, P. V. Narasimha Rao also became the first south Indian in history to govern India from Delhi. That too makes 1991 a milestone year.

Chapter 4

June: The Government

'The Mughals ruled India with the help of Kayasthas in their courts and administration. Even the Nizams of Hyderabad invited Kayasthas all the way from UP and paid them well for their services. So I decided I too must make the best use of them.'

That was how PV explained to my father his choice of Amar Nath Varma, an IAS officer of the Madhya Pradesh cadre, as his principal secretary. PV also decided to retain the cabinet secretary he inherited, Naresh Chandra, an IAS officer of the Rajasthan cadre, also a Kayastha. Having decided to keep the industries portfolio with himself, aware that he would have to undertake radical policy reforms, he retained Suresh Mathur, another Kayastha, as industries secretary.

The Kayastha community hails mainly from Uttar Pradesh, Bihar and Bengal. Since medieval times they've had a reputation as good administrators and record keepers. Thanks to their learning and administrative skills many Kayasthas acquired influential positions within the Mughal court and the imperial government of British India. The civil services remained their preferred career option through the post-Independence period. PV's familiarity with the Mathurs, Saxenas, Vermas, Nigams and Asthanas of

Hyderabad helped him relate to the Kayasthas of the north during his tenure in Delhi.

PV instinctively trusted his cabinet secretary and appreciated his wit and wisdom. After his stint as cabinet secretary, Chandra moved to the PMO as an adviser and tried to help PV deal with the Ayodhya issue. When PV chose to name him governor of Gujarat, BJP leader Atal Bihari Vajpayee was consulted and he immediately agreed. Chandra was India's ambassador to the United States during the Pokhran-II nuclear tests conducted by the Vajpayee government, and played a stellar role in defending and safeguarding Indian interests.

Varma was a very different kind of Kayastha. He neither had Chandra's gravitas nor his sense of humour. But he was a workhorse and knew how to get the government to move in the direction the prime minister wanted. He chaired the committee of secretaries with aplomb and authority and was known for his efficiency in 'getting things done'. Varma also fit the bill because he had served as secretary in the ministries of commerce and industry and at the Planning Commission. He was familiar with the policy advice being given by economists like Rakesh Mohan in industries, Jayanta Roy in commerce and Arvind Virmani in the Planning Commission. He also developed good rapport with Manmohan Singh and Montek Singh Ahluwalia.

Chandra and Varma had an uneasy equation but that is how a clever prime minister would want it to be. Creative tension among subordinate officials is what smart political bosses prefer. While PV inherited Chandra, Varma came on the recommendation of P. C. Alexander, Indira Gandhi's principal secretary in the early 1980s. PV relied greatly on Alexander's advice in the first few days of his prime ministership, and it was at his suggestion that

PV finally appointed Manmohan Singh as finance minister.

With his years of experience in the PMO, Alexander was able to help PV prepare a list of names for the council of ministers. As Indira Gandhi's virtual shadow after her return to power in 1980, he had intimate knowledge of Congress politics and leaders as well as the Nehru-Gandhi family. PV also consulted the files of the Intelligence Bureau on senior Congress leaders before deciding on his cabinet and the portfolio allocation.

After he was elected leader of the CPP on 20 June, PV settled down to the business of constituting his council of ministers. One of his first visitors was Cabinet Secretary Naresh Chandra, who handed over a detailed note on the economic situation. Chandra had been regularly briefing President Venkataraman on the economic situation. His office had a ready reckoner on all aspects of the economy that had also been prepared for off-the-record background briefings that Finance Secretary S. P. Shukla, Chief Economic Adviser Nayyar, Chandra himself and Principal Information Officer Ramamohan Rao would provide senior journalists.

PV was vaguely aware of the tenuous balance of payments situation but was surprised to read how bad it was. His predecessor had already taken the decision to mortgage gold in order to meet debt repayment obligations, pay for essential imports and avert default. Chandra's note spelt out in detail every challenge facing the economy.

'Is the situation this bad?' Chandra recalls PV asking him as he read the note.

'Sir, it is slightly worse,' replied Chandra, with his trademark smile. Even as the prime minister-to-be was engrossed in Chandra's note the cabinet secretary glanced at a sheet of paper on PV's table.

It seemed to be a list of names of senior Congressmen. Chandra knew that this was PV's list of potential members of his council of ministers. He was surprised, however, to note that the first name on the list was that of I. G. Patel.

Like Chandra Shekhar in November 1990, PV too first approached Patel and invited him to be the finance minister. Once again, IG declined.

PV had known IG, through friends, for even longer than Chandra Shekhar. Their link was Mohit Sen, the CPI theoretician, admirer of Indira Gandhi and friend of PV from their Hyderabad days. Mohit and IG were friends from their time together at Cambridge University, England, in the late 1940s. Mohit's association with PV was on account of his moving to Hyderabad in the 1960s after his marriage to another Cambridge contemporary, Vanaja Iyengar, a mathematics professor at Osmania University. Curiously, when Nehru died in 1964, the Hyderabad city Congress Party invited Mohit to address a condolence meeting along with PV, then a minister. Vanaja, Mohit, PV and IG were all known to my father and were familiar names at home from my school days onwards. Mohit had always held a sympathetic view of PV, and admired his commitment to land reforms. Now that PV was to be prime minister, Mohit was eager to be helpful. He strongly backed IG's name for the finance portfolio.

I don't know if PV was aware that IG was also Chandra Shekhar's first choice, but what may have gone in IG's favour as far as PV was concerned was the fact that among the available 'professional economists in government with an international reputation', as PV defined his potential finance minister, IG was the one person he knew who had handled the most recent loan negotiations with the IMF.

When Indira Gandhi had approached the IMF for balance of payments support in 1981, IG was governor of the RBI and, along with Finance Ministry officials and India's executive director on the IMF board, M. Narasimham, he had played an important role in dealing with the IMF and in lobbying hard with a large number of Western as well as developing countries.

As IG recalls, he had to travel around the world lobbying countries that had a say on the IMF board to secure their support for India's loan application. The US, which had veto power, was initially not supportive of India's application and wanted to impose stiffer conditionalities. IG had to lobby hard with a large number of Western and developing countries to ensure that India's loan application would get IMF board approval. PV was then external affairs minister and was keenly aware of IG's role and global influence. He also became acutely conscious of the nexus between geopolitics and economic policy choices.

PV was perhaps also aware of IG's career and policy orientation. As early as in 1986, while delivering the 15th Kingsley Martin Memorial Lecture in London, IG had called for 'a bonfire of industrial licensing'. Thanks to his stint at the London School of Economics, IG was well regarded in London. India had, after all, already decided to ship out gold bullion to the Bank of England to secure balance of payments support and PV knew more might have to be mortgaged.

Finally, PV was keen to ward off political aspirants for the job. We now know from Pranab Mukherjee's autobiography that Mukherjee had hoped to be included in PV's council of ministers and was dismayed at not being invited. The two had a good relationship and Mukherjee actively supported PV's candidacy for prime minister. PV was also under some pressure from Mukherjee's well-wishers to name him finance minister. PV could have given Mukherjee another portfolio, but chose not to induct him into the cabinet, instead naming him deputy chairman of the Planning Commission. Mukherjee neither had the backing of the Sonia coterie nor would PV have been too keen to induct someone who believed he was prime minister material. Unlike Arjun Singh, Mukherjee was not a member of the Lok Sabha. PV promised to offer an explanation, as Mukherjee puts it, saying 'Pranab, I cannot tell you why I did not take you into the Cabinet. Perhaps a day will come when I can speak to you about it.' Mukherjee regrets that the day never came.

Years later, when I was a professor at the Indian Council for Research in International Economic Relations (ICRIER) and IG was chairman of the governing board (PV was no longer prime minister), I asked him why he had turned down these offers. He offered a simple explanation. 'After years of living in Delhi and abroad I finally built a home in Baroda and had decided to live a quiet retired life there. I did not want to be seduced back to Delhi.' I believed him and my respect for him grew.

It is only after IG and PV passed away that I learnt that PV had approached IG a second time, inviting him again to join his council of ministers. Kalyani Shankar, a political journalist who knew PV well, believes he wanted to offer IG the commerce portfolio after P. Chidambaram had resigned in July 1992. On the other hand, PV's aide and media adviser Prasad does not rule out the possibility that PV wanted another economist in the government as a back-up just in case Dr Singh chose to quit, unable to deal with political attacks against him from within the Congress.

■

Once IG declined the first invitation, PV asked P. C. Alexander to suggest an alternative—he mentioned the name of Dr Manmohan Singh. PV approved the name and Alexander was asked to call Dr Singh.

Manmohan Singh had just returned from a trip abroad, landing in Delhi on the night of 20 June at an unearthly hour. He was woken up by Alexander on the morning of the 21st to be told that the prime minister wished to induct him as his finance minister. On 20th night, when PV called on President Venkataraman, he had sought the latter's advice on who should be named finance minister, adding that he would like to induct a professional economist. Venkataraman also suggested the names of IG and Manmohan Singh.

IG and Singh had led parallel lives. Both studied in Cambridge, England, both returned home to work in government, both were highly nationalistic in their orientation. While IG was known as 'Morarji's man', Singh was essentially 'Indira's man', having come into prominence in the early 1970s for his role in tackling high rates of inflation. Singh succeeded IG at the RBI. However, while IG chose to leave government and enter the world of academia, Singh moved from one government job to another, acquiring a reputation for diligence, trustworthiness and personal integrity.

Manmohan Singh took some time to transform himself from an honest civil servant into a canny politician. In his early days in government he earned the sobriquet of '1 per cent Singh' for declaring that he would bring the inflation rate down to 1 per cent. As finance minister he got into trouble with the Opposition in Parliament for announcing in his first budget speech that Rs 100 crore had been allocated for the Rajiv Gandhi Foundation. After all, the focus of the budget was on reducing public expenditure to tide over a crisis. The government was forced to roll back this pecuniary gesture to the slain leader's memory. Singh's bottom line was his concern for his personal reputation. Each time he was charged with sleeping at the wheel he would threaten to quit. PV had a difficult time handling his finance minister's thin skin, but stood by him all the way through. Dr Singh had offered to quit on at least three occasions in the face of intra-party criticism and each time PV had to get him to withdraw the resignation offer, reminding him that these attacks, mainly from Arjun Singh, A. K. Antony and the Congress left, were in fact aimed at the prime minister. The finance minister was but the surrogate target. On the third occasion when Singh sent in his resignation, an irritated PV sent word asking the finance minister to withdraw his resignation. The messenger was PV's aide, Prasad, who recalls the prime minister telling him, 'Dr Manmohan Singh is neither a full-fledged politician nor an officer... He does not understand that I am the target of their criticism. I can act against them, but I have to choose the right occasion and time. He is not bothered about such niceties. He says he is not a politician. How can he be a finance minister and still claim he is not a politician?'

A photograph that shows the two seated together with an eager Manmohan Singh looking into a preoccupied PV's face brings back memories of that historic photo of Nehru and Mahatma Gandhi. Gandhi made Nehru. PV made Manmohan. The latter acknowledged that handsomely at the time of PV's death, referring to him as his political mentor. When PV died, in 2004, Manmohan Singh attended every memorial meeting in New Delhi—the only member of the CWC to do so.

Having named Singh to the finance minister's job, PV never interfered with him. In 1993, when PV was coming under renewed attack from his own party, some of his aides suggested to him that he should bring an economist into the PMO and appear to be taking charge of economic policy. PV mulled the idea over. Curricula vitae were sought. The idea was then dropped. PV chose to stand by his finance minister.

In the initial months the finance minister worked with the team he had inherited, including Finance Secretary S. P. Shukla and Chief Economic Adviser Deepak Nayyar. Once the crisis and the danger of default had passed, PV gave the finance minister a free hand to select his own team to formulate the medium-term strategy that would involve entering into a structural adjustment and fiscal stabilization programme with the IMF and the World Bank. Later in the year Dr Singh brought in Montek Singh Ahluwalia as secretary, economic affairs, and Ashok Desai, a more pro-liberalization economist than Nayyar, as chief economic consultant. Dr Singh's team included several talented IAS officers like K. P. Geethakrishnan, Y. V. Reddy, N. K. Singh, D. Subbarao, Valluri Narayan and V. Govindarajan. Each of them had several years of experience working in the Finance Ministry at the centre and in their states. The only odd man out in this team was N. K. Singh whose experience had mainly been in the Ministry of Commerce. The rest were hard-core finance men. Two of them went on to become central bank governors.

The point about this entire narration is that PV was fully in charge of ministry making and it was his personal decision to appoint a reputed economist as his finance minister. Having done that, he let the finance minister pick his personnel, lending his political weight whenever PV's technocrat finance minister needed it.

Two years into his term, and under attack from anti-reform critics even within his own party, PV was advised again by a left-wing associate to diversify his economic advisers, replacing those with an IMF-World Bank background with those who were more left-of-centre. His response to the suggestion was in striking contrast to that of Manmohan Singh when the latter was criticized for replacing the left-of-centre Deepak Nayyar with the more pro-market economist, Ashok Desai. Singh was famously quoted as saying, 'The Finance Ministry is not a debating society'.

PV had a different reason for not changing the economists in government whom he had inherited from Rajiv Gandhi. He was told, he said to his interlocutor, that these economists were well regarded by the IMF and the World Bank, whose support he needed. He was also aware that some of them were 'well-connected to the Delhi elite', as he put it. He was also aware, he said, that the business media regarded them well. He needed the media's approval for his policies.

■

In their recently published accounts, some loyalists of the Nehru-Gandhi family have stated that Manmohan Singh was in fact Rajiv Gandhi's choice and that if Rajiv had become prime minister instead of PV, Singh would still have been the finance minister. One member of Sonia's coterie has gone to the extent of suggesting that Rajiv had even 'cleared IG Patel's name' for the finance minister's job!

All this afterthought on the part of the Nehru-Gandhi family loyalists is aimed at claiming family ownership for the personnel and policy choices that PV made in June 1991. Within the year PV got an opportunity to prove to the Nehru-Gandhi coterie that he was the boss. In July 1992, Commerce Minister Chidambaram, one of the ministers Rajiv first drafted into government, offered to quit following allegations of financial impropriety on his part in a matter pertaining to the ownership of shares in Fairgrowth Financial Services, a Bangalore-based company charged with involvement in a stock market scam.

Chidambaram believed he had done nothing wrong and was being politically targeted. He publicly offered to resign at a press conference. He had hoped that the prime minister would reject his offer and ask him to continue. This would have vindicated him. Most Congress MPs regarded Chidambaram as uppity and arrogant. That is partly a reflection of his demeanour. Tall and good looking, whether in his starched white veshti and crisp shirt or in jeans and T-shirt, Chidambaram wears his brilliance on his sleeve. He assumed the prime minister would turn his offer down.

PV was, however, very annoyed with Chidambaram. How could a minister go public with a resignation tendered in response to allegations of misconduct and then expect the prime minister to reject it, thereby giving him a clean chit? What did PV owe Chidambaram? Nothing. So the prime minister promptly accepted the minister's resignation. Chidambaram was stunned. More than a message to Chidambaram, it was a message to all his Cabinet colleagues—that they should not take the prime minister for granted.

The lesson was not fully learnt by all. In early January 1993, an Uzbekistan Airways plane had crash-landed in Delhi airport. The airport response was tardy and came in for widespread criticism.

Civil Aviation Minister Madhavrao Scindia, another close friend of Rajiv Gandhi's and a maharaja to boot, resigned his post, owning moral responsibility for the mishap and the mess-up. The prime minister promptly accepted his resignation. Scindia was flummoxed! PV was not inclined to accept the resignation but was irritated by the minister's bravado. He had sent word to Scindia asking him to withdraw his resignation. Scindia wanted the prime minister to reject it. That way he could occupy the high moral ground of having offered to quit and yet retain his job as an expression of respect for the prime minister. PV saw through the act, was not willing to grant him the halo, and so accepted the resignation. After these two incidents, every Congressman knew who the boss was.

PV also exercised his prime ministerial authority by the manner in which he appointed his senior officials. If he managed to acquire control of the IAS through Varma and Chandra, he underlined his role in foreign policy by appointing one of India's finest diplomats with a mind of his own, J. N. Dixit, as foreign secretary in December 1991. India's post–Cold War foreign policy as well as PV's outreach to Southeast and East Asia through his 'Look East Policy' and the fresh approach to West Asia defined by a new relationship with Israel were major diplomatic initiatives implemented by Dixit. In the PMO, he had a top-class China hand, Shyam Saran, as his joint secretary and a bright young diplomat, Ramu Damodaran, as his personal secretary. PV also counted on Ronen Sen, Rajiv Gandhi's closest diplomatic aide and someone who was au fait with Rajiv's key initiatives with the US, China, USSR and Pakistan. More importantly, Ronen became PV's go-to man for understanding the fast-paced changes in a crumbling Soviet Union, after the old guard at the Ministry of External Affairs let PV down with their dated assessments. In 1992 PV sent Ronen to Moscow to help establish strong links with a new Russia.

Each of PV's appointments strengthened the new government's ability to deal with the crisis at home and a rapidly changing world. I list these appointments to demonstrate that the political leadership of the day had the counsel of a talented and experienced set of administrators, economic policymakers and diplomats to negotiate a particularly difficult year. Astute political management on the part of the prime minister was key to a minority government's ability to manage an economic crisis amidst fundamental geopolitical changes. This aspect of crisis management and reform does not always get the attention it deserves.

PV once said to me that running a minority government for two full years was in itself a Herculean task. Even those with a parliamentary majority but heading multi-party coalitions had found the task unmanageable. But securing majority support for a minority government while simultaneously implementing some of the most radical policy reforms was a Himalayan achievement. For all that, PV took to the prime ministership effortlessly.

Chapter 5

July: The Reforms

A day after being sworn in as prime minister on the evening of 22 June, PV addressed the nation on television. His speech was drafted by Cabinet Secretary Naresh Chandra. Chandra recalls that he was assisted in this by Principal Information Officer Ramamohan Rao, though the latter very modestly claims the effort was entirely Chandra's and he has no recollection of his own role. Rao was a serving official of the Indian Information Service. He had cut his teeth as a wartime propagandist for the government in the 1962 conflict with China and reported from the battlefield during the 1965 war with Pakistan. He knew a thing or two about strategic communication during a crisis.

India was in a different kind of war, fighting on a different kind of battlefield. The prime minister was addressing the nation for the first time. He had to be seen speaking his mind. In his characteristic dull, dry and deadpan manner PV told his people:

> The economy is in a crisis. The balance of payments situation is exceedingly difficult. Inflationary pressures on the price level are considerable. There is no time to lose. The government and the country cannot keep living beyond

their means and there are no soft options left. We must tighten our belts and be prepared to make the necessary sacrifice to preserve our economic independence which is an integral part of our vision for a strong nation.

The prime minister then took an interesting step forward. Not restricting himself to crisis management, fiscal and balance of payments stabilization, PV chose to commit his government to wider economic reform.

The government is committed to removing the cobwebs that come in the way of rapid industrialization. We will work towards making India internationally competitive, taking full advantage of modern science and technology and opportunities offered by the evolving global economy.

In two simple sentences PV declared to the nation his decision to utilize the crisis as an opportunity to shift India's trade and industrial policy from the inward-orientation of the Nehru-Indira years onto a new trajectory of globally integrated development.

The 'evolving global economy' was being reshaped by new geopolitical factors—the disintegration of the Soviet Union and the restructuring of the world trading system by an assertive United States. It was the US that had helped create the GATT in the 1950s with the purpose of installing a global trading regime that would enable the war-torn economies of Europe and Asia to rebuild themselves while creating new markets for US exports. The US believed GATT had served its purpose, helping Germany, Japan and many 'East Asian Tigers' emerge as globally competitive economies. Their exports were now threatening the US and the sole superpower wanted a restructuring of the global trading system, replacing GATT with a new world trade organization.

Opinion was already divided in India between those who sought to tackle the balance of payments crisis through 'import-compression' and those who felt the crisis was an opportunity to open up the economy and seek export–oriented investment that would increase India's export earnings.

On his very first day as prime minister, PV told the nation that he would like to see India take advantage of the evolving global economy, rather than shut its doors tighter. While the immediate demands of crisis management, especially the urgent need to avoid default on external debt repayments, required 'import compression', in the months to come PV lent his weight to trade liberalization and the reintegration of the Indian economy with the global, especially the dynamic East Asian economies.

The second significant statement he had made was about making India 'internationally competitive'. Every graduate student of economics knows that for an economy to be internationally competitive it must contain sectors that operate at competitive levels of scale and efficiency. One of the worst legacies of the licence–permit raj was to restrict firm and plant size. Joint secretaries in Udyog Bhavan decided the capacity of firms, neither the market nor technology.

To become globally competitive Indian industry needed to exploit what economists call the 'economies of scale'—building large plants that cater to a global and not just a local market. The philosophy behind curbing scale was shaped by concern about monopolistic and oligopolistic practices of large firms. To 'prevent the concentration of economic power' in any given industry was a stated objective of industrial policy.

This did not mean that every company strictly adhered to government regulations. All it meant was that such restrictions encouraged corruption. Companies would operate at scales well beyond their authorized capacity and sell the excess output in the black market. Inspectors and taxmen would be bribed. For a firm, this made economic sense. Indeed, this is how many globally competitive firms had been set up. What PV decided he would do was to bring them out of the closet, so to speak: Legalize capacity by removing regulations that delegitimized expansion of scale.

Few seemed to notice the radical implications of that sentence in the prime minister's very first speech. It set the stage for the profound transformation of industrial policy that PV authorized a month later.

■

But first things first. The government's immediate task was to avoid default. It was not just the ignominy associated with a default that India wished to avoid. The loss of confidence in a country's ability to manage its economy prudently is not easily reversed.

'I was not concerned about the reaction of the common man,' PV once told me, 'the sympathy of the common man is always with the debtor. In all our films, people sympathize with the one who mortgages his family silver. The villain is always the lender.'

PV's predecessor had already taken the decision that India would rather mortgage gold than default on external payments. PV authorized a second round of gold mortgage. The first tranche, undertaken in May 1991, involved the shipment of 20 tonnes of gold. The second round, undertaken in July 1991, involved the movement of around 46.91 tonnes of gold, valued at US$405 million, from the RBI vaults in Bombay to the vaults of the

Bank of England in London.

In his account of the gold transaction, Rangarajan writes about the moments of drama during the movement of the second instalment of gold. The RBI had ensured what Rangarajan calls 'vault to vault' insurance of the gold consignment. As those nearly 47 tonnes of gold moved from Bombay's Mint Road to a secluded spot at Sahar airport, the van containing the gold was under constant security surveillance, just like in a Hollywood movie. The already nervous officials and security guards handling the entire operation had some truly tense moments when a loud bang made the convoy stop to check if a tyre had burst. 'Before much commotion could happen,' recalls Rangarajan, 'the convoy resumed.' The journalist Shankkar Aiyar got wind of the gold airlift and earned his professional brownie points reporting it.

But even as dollars were earned mortgaging gold, dollars were lost as NRIs continued to transfer funds to banks abroad. Given that the priority for the government was to avert external default, there was no other option but to further tighten import controls. The import squeeze began to hurt the economy which, on the one hand, slowed down, and, on the other, experienced inflationary pressure on the price level. The economy was in the throes of what economists define as stagflation.

Opinion was divided within the government on whether 'import-compression' ought to be ensured through physical controls, that is, an outright ban, or ensured through price signals, that is, the devaluation of the rupee. Finance Minister Manmohan Singh tilted in favour of using the exchange rate rather than import bans. Over the financial year 1990-91 the rupee had already depreciated by around 11 per cent, but it was now felt that a one-time sharp adjustment would stabilize the rupee by renewing confidence in it. On 1 July, the rupee was devalued by around 9 per cent and on 3 July there was a further devaluation by around 11 per cent, with the adjustment working out to a 17.38 per cent devaluation. The rupee slipped from Rs 17.9 to a US dollar to Rs 24.5. By the end of 1992 it was approximately Rs 31 to a dollar, and remained around that level till the end of PV's term.

The entire exercise was dubbed 'hop, skip and jump' by Singh and Rangarajan. It was a game the two played in secrecy. But while Singh had secured the prime minister's authorization, PV developed cold feet after the first step, on 1 July. Devaluation was a bad word in Indian politics. PV would have known of the 1966 devaluation episode and how Indira Gandhi had been criticized for it. Not many are aware that when Indira devalued the rupee in 1966, again under IMF advice, she took care to depute officials from the PMO and Finance Ministry to several state capitals so that important chief ministers were briefed about it. A sudden change in the value of the rupee had to be politically managed. It was not just an economic decision.

So when PV's critics attacked the government for the first step devaluation, the prime minister advised the finance minister to hold back the second step. But Singh, who was familiar with the 1966 episode (the economists who handled it were all his mentors or friends—K. N. Raj, I. G. Patel, D. R. Gadgil, Jagdish Bhagwati, P. N. Dhar and Manu Shroff), decided that if the second step was not taken as planned it might never be taken.

'The first step was to test the waters,' Manmohan Singh recently revealed. 'So although there was opposition to the move, it was manageable. So I said that by July 3 [1991], we must complete the full thing. C. Rangarajan was the Deputy Governor [of RBI]... Prime Minister Narasimha Rao had doubts over the second instalment of the exchange rate adjustment and told me, in fact, to stop it. But when I called up Rangarajan, he said that he had already shot the goal.'

Once the two-step action was taken, government spokespersons moved fast to assure the markets that there would be no further devaluation. The rupee had found its warranted level. The markets stabilized.

Following devaluation, the government began the process of liberalizing the trade regime, moving away from India's traditional export pessimism to a new philosophy that viewed exports as another source of growth as well as a source of foreign exchange. India is a resources-deficient economy in per capita terms, and was vitally dependent on oil imports. It needed to finance not just essential imports but also export-promoting imports in sectors using new technologies.

No sooner had the devaluation exercise been completed, PV moved on the trade policy front, authorizing an end to the sop given to exporters called the Cash Compensatory System (CCS). The CCS was a subsidy given to exporters to compensate for all the inefficiencies of the Indian system that made exports globally uncompetitive. Devaluation was an incentive for exporters. Hence, on the same day that the RBI took the second step on rupee devaluation, the CCS was withdrawn, ignoring the apprehensions of the Commerce Ministry, which has long regarded its dharma to be the defence of the interests of exporters.

On 3 July, instructed by PV, Singh called in Commerce Minister Chidambaram and Commerce Secretary Montek Singh Ahluwalia and instructed them to prepare papers abolishing CCS and get the prime minister's signature. Singh told them that with the rupee devalued the government could afford to displease exporters by withdrawing this subsidy. The politician in Chidambaram balked at the idea. Singh had to then tell the commerce minister that the prime minister wanted the orders issued the same day. By the end of the day CCS was abolished. In an interview given to the *Economic Times* a few days later Chidambaram defended his action saying, 'There can be no birth without birth pangs.'

Trade policy reform was defined by two key considerations: first, to enable India to move closer to the emerging new global trade policy architecture that was to be put in place by the yet to be established World Trade Organization; second, to link import entitlements to export performance. The bureaucratic system of the government granting import licences was replaced by a market mechanism that would enable exporters to earn 'exim scrips' that could then be traded on the market. Importers would then be able to buy the scrips and pay for their imports. This was a transitional arrangement that sought to ensure better trade balance.

Combining devaluation with trade policy liberalization made sense. The purpose of taking these measures was also to demonstrate to international investors and financial institutions that the new minority government was prepared to take difficult decisions. Thus the measures were aimed as much at boosting confidence in India as they were at securing access to hard currency.

A week after the devaluation exercise and on the eve of the first session of Parliament, PV addressed the nation for a second time. In a speech televised on 9 July, he explained to the people in simple terms the logic behind his early policy moves. You cannot import if you do not export. 'My motto is—trade, not aid. Aid is a crutch. Trade builds pride. India has been trading for thousands of years.' He then went on to emphasize that he intended to go beyond crisis management to bring India in line with the rest of the world. 'We believe that India has much to learn from what is happening elsewhere in the world. Many countries are bringing in far-reaching changes. We find major economic transformation sweeping large countries like the Soviet Union and China… There is a change in outlook, a change in mindset everywhere. India too cannot lag behind if she has to survive, as she must, in the new environment.'

Within a fortnight of taking charge as prime minister, and even before the first sitting of Parliament, PV took momentous decisions that helped restore confidence in the economy. The next major step, and the one that the IMF and the rating agencies were eagerly looking forward to, was a sharp reduction in the fiscal deficit. If exchange rate management was the RBI's job, fiscal management was the finance minister's.

In fact, the single most important announcement made in Singh's first budget speech, on 24 July 1991, was the reduction in the budget deficit. It was a commitment that Yashwant Sinha had first made in December 1990. It was now Manmohan Singh's turn to deliver on that commitment. The fiscal deficit was brought down sharply from a high of 8.4 per cent of GDP in 1990-91 to 5.9 per cent in 1991-92. The Seventh Plan average was as high as 8.2 per cent. This was, by any standard, a sharp and decisive cut.

Reducing the fiscal deficit by 2 percentage points of GDP meant reducing government expenditure greatly. In the long run a government's deficit can also be reduced by raising revenues. But the crisis and the IMF's conditions for extending balance of payments support required a surgical cut in expenditure in one go. Singh was candid in his budget speech: 'The crisis of the fiscal system is a cause for serious concern... Without decisive action now, the situation will move beyond the possibility of corrective action.' He proposed a steep reduction in subsidies—food, fertilizer and exports—and also reduced spending on defence, all aimed at bringing the fiscal deficit down.

Manmohan Singh's budget speech has become a landmark policy statement. His detailed explanation of the origins of the balance of payments and fiscal crisis, his defence of government response and his proposals for reform were spelt out clearly but in his usual soft-spoken manner. The Lok Sabha heard him out in silence. The press and visitors' galleries were full. The nation watched him on television as he summed up his long thirty-one-page speech of over 18,000 words with the dire warning that a 'grave economic crisis' faced the country but that the government would take 'determined action'.

The last paragraph of that historic budget speech has since been etched in the minds of successive generations of economic policymakers:

> Sir, I do not minimise the difficulties that lie ahead on the long and arduous journey on which we have embarked. But as Victor Hugo once said, 'no power on earth can stop an idea whose time has come.' I suggest to this august House that the emergence of India as a major economic power in the world happens to be one such idea. Let the whole world hear it loud and clear. India is now wide awake. We shall prevail. We shall overcome.

Exchange rate adjustment and fiscal deficit reduction would in themselves have been enough to win the confidence of credit rating agencies and financial markets. However, PV went a step further. Intervening in the debate on the motion of thanks to the president for his address to Parliament, on 15 July, PV claimed, 'All [our] measures were really written about in newspapers times without number...So it is not as if the measures which we have taken have just dropped from the [heavens] overnight... People are more knowledgeable than myself on what is happening in the Soviet Union... We cannot keep out of this change, this complete global sweeping change that is coming.'

It is with this perspective in mind that PV instructed the Ministry of Industry (of which he was then the cabinet minister) to prepare a new industrial policy dismantling the infamous licence-permit raj.

■

As we know, Jawaharlal Nehru was personally involved in drafting the First and Second Industrial Policy Resolutions of 1948 and 1956. Indira Gandhi unveiled her version of an even more state-directed industrial development policy in 1973. By the mid-1980s there was sufficient intellectual opinion in favour of ending this regime of controls and licences. It was widely acknowledged that instead of fulfilling the stated objectives of ushering in a 'socialistic pattern of society' or reducing monopolistic and oligopolistic practices, governmental regulations were only perpetuating inefficiency and promoting corruption. These were policies which prevented Indian firms from becoming globally competitive, which kept foreign investment away in the name of promoting domestic business, which required entrepreneurs taking business risks to first secure permission of a joint secretary in the Ministry of Industry, with the official concerned having no clue about the risks involved or the opportunities available; which told firms where to invest, how to invest, how much to invest, etc.

Both Rajiv Gandhi and V. P. Singh understood the need to dismantle the licence-permit raj, but neither had the political courage to do so. PV chose to bite the bullet. Under the leadership of the prime minister, principal secretary A. N. Varma, a group of officials from the PMO, and the Industries Ministry (with the economic adviser in the ministry, Rakesh Mohan, playing a key role), put together a new industrial policy statement that would be unveiled on 24 July along with the government's first budget policy. Varma and Mohan had a policy draft ready from their time together in the Industries Ministry in V. P. Singh's government.

On 12 July, the *Hindustan Times* carried a report by its political editor, Kalyani Shankar, declaring 'Industrial Licensing to Go'. Those of us who knew that Shankar had direct access to PV saw this report as being aimed at testing political waters. Quite understandably, PV's critics accused him of departing from Nehru's policies. PV then instructed his aides to quote copiously from Nehru in defence of his policy action. After paying ritual obeisance to Nehru and Indira and the contribution of their policies to India's industrialization, the statement of 24 July dismantled in one fell swoop the bureaucratic edifice their regimes had erected in the name of socialism. In typical PV style, he made P. J. Kurien, a junior minister, announce this radical policy change hours before Singh's first budget speech.

The drama around this historic decision has been narrated in detail by Jairam Ramesh, a PMO functionary at the time. It was PV's intention to follow up the trade policy reforms of 4 July with industrial policy reforms in the run-up to the budget. The news that important industrial policy changes were on the anvil were reported during that week in several newspapers. However, at the cabinet meeting on 19 July there was resistance to PV's initiatives. He was the industries minister and the opposition came from his detractors, led by Arjun Singh. PV immediately proposed the creation of a cabinet sub-committee, a Group of Ministers (GoM), that included his loyalists, the external affairs minister, Madhavsinh Solanki, communications minister, Rajesh Pilot, and petroleum minister, B. Shankaranand; Sonia loyalist Fotedar (he was minister for health and family welfare and so had no role at all in making industrial policy, but was inducted to ensure the support of Sonia loyalists); pro-reform ministers Manmohan Singh and Chidambaram; and the prime minister's critics, Arjun Singh and Balram Jakhar.

Jairam Ramesh helped get the statement on industrial policy cleared by the GoM and the CWC by adding a long preamble that paid generous homage to Jawaharlal Nehru, the architect of the 1948 and 1956 industrial policy resolutions; Indira Gandhi, who made changes in policy through the industrial policy reforms of 1973, 1977 and 1980; and to policy changes brought about by Rajiv Gandhi in 1985 and 1986. All the party gods had been propitiated. The motto was 'change with continuity'. PV appreciated Ramesh's spin doctoring. As Ramesh recalls, 'Varma [principal secretary to the prime minister] called me and said that Narasimha Rao was appreciative of what I had done and felt that, with the preamble, we might still be able to get the industrial policy reforms through.'

Finally, as I have mentioned, the much delayed 'big bang' of industrial delicensing and decontrol was announced by Minister of State for Industry P. J. Kurien on the morning of the finance minister's budget speech on 24 July. Given the political and media focus on the budget speech, the real reform of the day did not get the play it deserved. This was clearly by design.

Not only was the media focus on the budget, but even the Opposition chose to target budgetary proposals more than this radical policy shift. It was only after a fortnight that *India Today* journalists Sudeep Chakravarti and R. Jagannathan got the picture right when they reported:

> Here is something that Rajiv Gandhi forgot to do as Prime Minister. He talked about taking India into the 21st century but forgot all about the present one and the opposition it may have to the future. P V Narasimha Rao and his finance minister Manmohan Singh got it just right. On the one hand, they sang praises about Nehruvian socialism. On the other hand, they took the country by the scruff of the neck and said move, or we all die.

The early emergency measures of July were followed up by more sustained efforts at economic liberalization, industrial policy reform and fiscal stabilization in the months to come. In September, the government issued an ordinance removing restrictions on capacity expansion, mergers, acquisitions, amalgamation and takeovers that had all been closely controlled till then by the Monopolies and Restrictive Trade Practices Act of 1969.

By November, the finance minister was able to seal a deal with the World Bank for financing under its enhanced structural adjustment facility (ESAF) and another with the IMF for a standby loan of US$2.2 billion. As foreign exchange reserves kept rising, some of the more draconian import curbs were eased and procedures for foreign investment relaxed. By February of 1992, PV was able to travel to the World Economic Forum at Davos, the annual gathering of business and government leaders, and reassure the world that India was back in business.

■

In October 1991, IMF managing director Michel Camdessus called on Prime Minister Narasimha Rao. PV had only one message for him. 'I am willing to do whatever is good for the economy, as long as not one worker tells me he has lost his job because of me.'

In the media and in political discourse that approach came to be defined as 'structural adjustment with a human face' and 'reforms with a human face'. In his classic treatise on the reforms of 1991 and what they say about a changing India, business historian Gurcharan Das sees PV's 'reforms with a human face' formulation as evidence of his being a 'reluctant liberaliser' who lacked faith in reforms and was unable to view his policies as 'pro-poor' in themselves. 'A reformer would have known that the reforms are the only hope for the poor', says Das.

In the long run, maybe so. PV's focus, like that of any politician, was not on the distant future. His immediate objective was to see that no trade union would bring workers onto the streets protesting job losses caused by reforms. He chose to retain additional charge of the Ministry of Consumer Affairs, Civil Supplies and Public Distribution, along with industries, through 1991-92 (he handed this ministry over to his left-wing critic A. K. Antony only in 1993), to make sure that he remained as focused on the 'human face' as he was on structural adjustment.

PV went a step further. In his famous and thoughtful address to the April 1992 AICC session at Tirupati, PV dwelt at length on this issue.

There is one danger which we must recognize and guard against in the 'opening up' process... This could lead to wider disparities within society. To meet this situation, we have to enable the under-privileged sections also to derive the benefit of the new opportunities. This process would naturally need some time to fructify. Until that happens, there has to be a by-pass arrangement whereby benefits reach the lowest rungs of the social pyramid directly from the State. We are doing this.

That by-pass arrangement took the form of an employment guarantee scheme, increased funding for social welfare programmes and increased investment in rural development. An IAS officer of the Andhra Pradesh cadre, intellectually left-of-centre, K. R. Venugopal, was made responsible for monitoring these initiatives.

■

In the monsoon months of 1992 I had sought an appointment with PV. I wanted to interview him for the *Economic Times*. Prasad, the prime minister's press secretary, suggested that I fly with him on a day trip he was making to Aurangabad and chat with him en route.

PV had been prime minister for more than a year. How did he assess his year in office? PV told me that he felt a sense of satisfaction. He had managed to get a grip on the economy. The medium-term programme with the IMF had been wrapped up. The rupee had stabilized. The bitter medicine of fiscal adjustment had been administered. Next year, he hoped, the government would have the money to increase spending on social welfare, health and education. In the first year, fiscal stabilization was the priority.

He was also satisfied that he had been able to take the Congress along in pushing through economic liberalization. He spoke at length, defending decontrol, delicensing and the steps he had taken to promote private enterprise—both domestic and foreign. He reminded me that apart from the industries portfolio he had also decided to hold additional charge of the Ministry of Civil Supplies, Consumer Affairs and Public Distribution to ensure that the government was responsive to concerns about inflation and would deliver food to the poor through the public distribution system to compensate for the inflationary pressures generated by the devaluation of the rupee and high oil prices.

'Whatever I have done conforms to the views of Rajiv Gandhi. It also fits into the thinking of Panditji. After all, he too spoke of India being a "mixed economy". You know, I used to tell Vithal [my father], I have always quoted Panditji in my defence!'

I was aware of that because when PV asked my father to help draft his presidential address to the Tirupati session of the AICC, in April 1992, he explicitly instructed him to liberally quote from Nehru in defence of his policies (see Appendix).

PV's real contribution to economic reform and liberalization was his political management of a contentious process. During one of my meetings with him after he stepped down as prime minister, in April 1997, PV clarified that he was aware of Rajiv Gandhi's views on economic policies and he walked a path that Rajiv too would have taken, if he had been prime minister. PV summed up, 'It is because we had a clear idea of the problem and what had to be done that we were able to move so quickly and deal with the situation.'

Over a year later, in early 1999, I called on PV to pick his brains for a paper I was commissioned to write for a conference organized by the economist S. L. Rao, at the time chairman of the Central Electricity Regulatory Authority and of the national management forum of the All India Management Association. The focus of S. L. Rao's conference was 'managing the Indian state' and he wanted me to write on the political management of economic reforms in India. By that time several seminars and conferences had already been held in India and abroad on India's reforms. Economists were busy claiming credit for things that worked and apportioning blame for mistakes made. A new folklore was being generated about the heroes and villains of India's economic saga. New theories were being propounded about 'reform by stealth,' 'reform under pressure' and 'reform by a technocratic elite'.

PV followed all this closely, reading journals, newspapers and magazines. He was amused by it all. All the talented and committed economists and civil servants in government could not have pushed reforms without political support.

'Yes, there were times I was guided by Manmohan and the other economists,' PV told me. 'There were also times I had to push Manmohan and others. I had to tell them I will take the political responsibility. You go ahead.'

PV took an avuncular approach to Singh. PV was seventy, Singh was fifty-nine. PV had lived through the rough and tumble of politics, Singh had had a smooth career in government, rising through the ranks over two decades. Both had been left-of-centre in their ideological orientation till the 1980s and then moved with the times. As the world changed, so did their thinking about it. Singh was always deferential towards PV and PV reciprocated that regard.

When PV sent his aide, Prasad, to get Singh to withdraw

his resignation on the third occasion when the finance minister was provoked by critics into doing so, PV reminded Prasad, 'Dr Manmohan Singh is allergic to politicians. That is why I cannot send a politician to persuade him.'

PV believed there were at least three reasons why Rajiv Gandhi had not been able to push major reforms during his tenure: first, the Congress party leadership was not convinced that reforms were the right step and Rajiv failed to win them over. Arjun Singh, A. K. Antony, N. D. Tiwari, among others, actively opposed PV's initiatives too. Second, Rajiv's initiatives were seen as 'pro-rich' and 'pro-business', not as reforms. His Doon School background, his corporate friends and his widely publicized holidays added to that image. The dramatic collapse of support for the Congress between the elections of 1984 and 1989 proves the point. Third, the Congress Party had become far too centralized in its functioning, while the implementation of far-reaching reforms required greater political decentralization, given that regional parties had gained ascendance over the Congress in developed states like Punjab, Haryana, Tamil Nadu, Andhra Pradesh, Karnataka, and Gujarat.

Ownership of change from below was essential. But many in the Congress at the state level would only support initiatives because they got instructions from the high command, not because they felt such initiatives would strengthen their own political base and widen their constituency of support. PV made it a point to secure the support of regional non-Congress leaders for his initiatives.

The ideas were not new, PV would say. All the reports advocating change—by L. K. Jha, Abid Hussain, M. Narasimham, P. C. Alexander—had been presented to Indira and Rajiv. He was familiar with that thinking. PV summed it up for me, 'The political leadership had access to all these ideas. The challenge was not in making announcements and implementing their recommendations. It was in creating the political climate in which they could get implemented.'

■

The idea that the licence-permit raj had become a constraint on industrial growth and economic development was not new. Among the first to propagate that view were the distinguished economist couple Jagdish Bhagwati and Padma Desai. Their widely read book, *India: Planning for Industrialization*, published as early as in 1970, was critical of governmental controls on the growth of firms and drew attention to their negative impact on industrial development. Indira Gandhi's economic advisers frowned on these views till professional economists began to worry about the slowdown in the pace of industrial and economic growth.

For half a century before Independence the economy of British India remained virtually stagnant with an average rate of growth close to zero per cent per annum. In the 1950s and 1960s the economy grew at around 3.5 to 4 per cent, and slowed down to around 3 per cent in the 1970s. The average annual rate of growth between 1950 and 1980 was 3.5 per cent. In the 1980s the economy perked up and grew at around 5.5 per cent. The Green Revolution of the 1970s and rising rural incomes had unlocked what economists called the 'demand constraint' on growth that had contributed to a slowing down of the economy in the 1960s and early 1970s. It had also unleashed new enterprise in rapidly growing regions of peninsular India. Investments made over the years in social and economic infrastructure contributed to an increase in labour productivity and an improvement in the output-capital ratio. Consequently, economic growth began to accelerate once again.

There are those who believe the Indian economy began looking up at least a decade before 1991. The disputation about the dating of the economy's turnaround is as much about data and estimation methodologies as it is about personalities. The proponents of greater economic openness argued that Indira Gandhi was not committed to a change of economic direction away from the bureaucratic socialism that she inherited and further consolidated in her time. They charged Indira's 'left-oriented' and 'statist' economists with preventing a change of economic direction even after China changed tracks in the late 1970s.

On the other hand, Indira loyalists would assert that the move away from Nehruvian socialism began during the Emergency (1975-77) was taken forward by Morarji Desai and his Janata Party government in 1977-79, and finally accelerated after Indira Gandhi's return to power in 1980. Her decision to enter into a borrowing programme with the IMF in 1980 has been cited as evidence of a change of gear and direction by Indira Gandhi herself. Thus, for example, Arjun Sengupta, an economic adviser in Indira Gandhi's PMO and a member of the Planning Commission in PV's government, would claim prior ownership of the ideas that came to define the policy shift of 1991, while differentiating the 1980s brand of reform from that of Manmohan Singh and his team in 1991.

Prime Minister Morarji Desai tried to take the first step towards creating a political consensus in favour of economic liberalization by appointing a high-powered committee chaired by a highly respected economic journalist, Vadilal Dagli, then editor of the pro-liberalization business newsmagazine, *Commerce*. The Dagli committee fired the first salvo, drawing attention to the fact that many controls on industry had been imposed by the British imperial government during the Second World War and had long outlived their purpose; that the government's subsidy bill was rising rapidly while many of the subsidies doled out either did not serve their purpose or had negative economic consequences; and that there were lots of laws on the statute books that were no longer relevant to the needs of the day and needed to simply be terminated. While the report did not call for a 'bonfire of controls', as IG would years later, the Desai government fell even before the report's submission.

Indira Gandhi did encourage new thinking on economic policy. During her tenure and that of Rajiv Gandhi more committees were constituted to prepare reports that would advocate a further easing of governmental controls, administrative reform and liberalization of economic activity. However, neither really acted on the recommendations of most of these committees, and it was left to PV to walk the talk.

Much ink has been spilled by economists duelling in professional journals on the vital matter of dating the turn in India's economic fortunes. Understandably so, since many professional reputations and careers have been constructed on the basis of rival claims about who was the saviour!

Interestingly, opinion is divided among economists who now serve the Narendra Modi government. Chief Economic Adviser Arvind Subramanian and RBI Governor Raghuram Rajan (who recently demitted office) had, in their academic avatar, pre-government, taken the view closer to that of Arjun Sengupta. In their view economic reforms began in the early 1980s and it is that decade which constitutes a turning point for the India growth story. The vice chairman of NITI Aayog, Arvind Panagariya has, however, offered a four-period classification of India's growth transitions and identifies 1987-88 as the tipping point when the economy moved from an average annual rate of growth of around 4.8 per cent to 'six per cent plus'.

Recognizing the significance of changes in both economic policy and performance in the 1980s Panagariya concludes, 'To be sure, the growth rate shifted in the early 1980s, but only to the modest rate of 4.8 per cent (from 3.2 in 1965-81). The shift to the 6 per cent plus rate did not take place until the late 1980s.'

More than the differences about the magnitude and timing of the shift in the growth rate, there have also been disagreements among these economists on whether the reforms of the 1980s and even of the 1990s were merely 'pro-business' without being 'pro-market'. In other words, did reforms benefit the business class more than the consumer by liberalizing policy without encouraging greater competition? While Subramaniam takes this view, Panagariya dismisses it as a 'spurious distinction', arguing that liberalization had in fact removed the barriers to entry of new firms.

While economists and statisticians argue about data, it is important to understand that 1991 was not just another year for the economy. It was a manifestation of all the mistakes India's political leaders and policymakers had made in the preceding decades and it was the year in which expectations about India changed dramatically. For all the so-called changes in policy and performance in the 1980s, the union finance ministry's own annual *Economic Survey* of February 1990 drew attention to at least four significant weaknesses in the economy: a low savings rate, high fiscal deficit, a widening balance of payments gap and inadequate growth in employment:

> The next year is the first year of the Eighth Plan. The critical
> tasks at this stage are to design an employment oriented
> development strategy that combines growth with equity,
> a trade policy that aims at rapid export growth so as to
> reduce the external payments deficit and a fiscal policy that
> increases savings and contains inflationary pressures.

The *Survey's* overall tone was neither celebratory about an
improved economic performance in the Seventh Plan period,
nor was there a call to arms for radical changes in policy in
the Eighth Plan. No one reading that anxious account of India's
economic woes would have had positive expectations about the
country's economic performance in the 1990s.

Expectations shape outcomes in a world of uncertainty.
Expectations about the economy end up being self-fulfilling
prophecies. If you expect tomorrow to be better than today, you
take economic decisions that ensure that tomorrow is indeed better.
If, on the other hand, one believes the future to be bleaker than
the present, one ends up taking decisions and making choices
that contribute to a less than satisfactory outcome.

The policy changes and the gradual improvement in economic
performance in the 1980s did not alter the 'state of expectations',
so to speak, about where India was headed as dramatically as the
'big bang' of 1991. Much of the growth spurt in the 1980s was
enabled by an increase in public investment and expenditure which,
in turn, led to the fiscal crisis of the late 1980s. On the other
hand, the policy shifts in 1991-92 triggered positive expectations
about future growth, stimulating private investment.

Travelling to Davos in February 1992, and describing the

World Economic Forum as an 'Economic Mecca', PV spoke at length to his audience of global CEOs about the new post-Cold War world and India's role in it 'as an economically dynamic and politically stable' democracy. He assured his Davos audience that his policy initiatives were irreversible and would be taken forward because the change underway in India was evolutionary, not revolutionary.

A debate has also raged over the years whether the reforms and liberalization of policy in 1991 were 'home-grown' or 'imposed' by an external actor—the IMF. It is true that many of the policies implemented in and after 1991 had been advocated by various expert committees of the government of India through the 1980s. PV did nothing in 1991 that had not already been suggested by someone or the other at home. To that extent they were home-grown. But it is also true that the implementation of many of these reforms was a policy conditionality imposed by the IMF as a quid pro quo for the balance of payments support India sought from it.

Apart from the IMF, the World Bank and several donor country governments also made their own policy demands. Finally, it is also a fact that not everything advocated by the expert committees, the IMF, World Bank and donor governments was implemented. PV picked and chose what he felt he could reasonably defend within his own party and Parliament. It was his 'middle way'.

It is useful to remember that it suited both the critics and the defenders of economic liberalization and reform to point to an external actor as the inspiration for change. The critics, both the Communists and the BJP, sought to stoke nationalist anger against a government that they depicted as succumbing to 'imperialist' (as the Communists would say) or 'foreign' (as BJP would argue) pressure.

A highly regarded Marxist ideologue told me at the time that in India mobilizing public opinion against a policy was easier when that policy was shown to be imposed by 'imperialist powers' rather than domestic political leaders. Given the legacy of the national movement, public opinion was still suspicious of Western powers. In a fractious democracy like India few would see local political leaders as being so powerful as to pursue policies that were being so virulently attacked. As for those advocates of reform who also pointed a finger at external actors, it was an easy way of not accepting responsibility for their actions just in case things did not go the way they were expected or hoped to.

In 1992 the Left Front took out a rally in New Delhi against the economic policies of the Narasimha Rao government. A large crowd gathered on Delhi's Boat Club lawns between India Gate and Vijay Chowk. The newly arrived resident representative of the IMF in India, Armando Linde, called me at my office in Times House. Linde was a Cuban American, an IMF economist, and was responsible for overseeing the implementation of the IMF programme in India. He was curious. Would it be safe to drive around Delhi, Linde asked.

I assured him that Indian communists who had opted for the parliamentary path were a peaceful lot. He was keen to go down to Rajpath and watch the rally. I volunteered to take him there. I drove down to his home-cum-office in Lutyens' Delhi and we drove to Boat Club lawns. Parking our car on a side street we walked towards the rally. Dozens of protestors held placards saying, 'Down with IMF', 'IMF Go Back' and other such slogans.

Why blame the IMF, Linde asked me. 'Your government is not even listening to us properly. They want to do only what they can.' It was Linde who narrated to me what Camdessus had been told by PV: that the government would be happy to accept all good advice from the IMF as long as 'not one worker is out of employment' due to those policies.

I told Linde about India's national movement and how it was still easier for a politician to justify unpopular policies by blaming the foreigner. 'Just like my cousins in Cuba,' he said, and added, 'Why blame only the IMF? They can at least add the World Bank's name to their placards!'

■

The top twenty companies in India, defined by market capitalization, in 1990 were no different from the top twenty in 1980. The only major entrant during the decade was Dhirubhai Ambani's Reliance Industries. The rest were names that generations of Indians had grown up with. Firms belonging to business houses like the Tatas, Birlas, Bajajs and multinational firms like Hindustan Unilever and Nestlé. The 1990s were different.

If in 1990, Tata Steel, Tata Motors, Century Textiles and Grasim (Birlas) and Mafatlals were among the top ten, by 2000 all of them had slipped down the assets ladder, yielding place to Azim Premji's Wipro, Narayana Murthy's Infosys, Ambani's Reliance, Subhash Chandra's Zee Entertainment and Shiv Nadar's HCL Technologies. Change in the Indian business scene was not just at the top. The 1990s was the decade of churning in India's corporate sector. Unshackled from the infamous licence-permit raj, first generation entrepreneurs made the most of new business opportunities.

Economic liberalization made it easier for new business groups across the country to grow. The licence-permit raj of the Indira era in fact facilitated the growth of oligopolies and crony capitalists, especially the Delhi-, Bombay-, Calcutta- and Chennai-based big business houses. Many government reports made this point. What delicensing did was to make it easier for new business groups to flourish, especially those based in new centres of industrial activity like Gujarat, Karnataka, Andhra Pradesh and Punjab-Haryana. The regional dispersal of business activity was an important motivator and consequence of economic liberalization. Apart from the 'children of reform', as Manmohan Singh once called them, like Narayana Murthy and Azim Premji of the information technology services business, new business leaders like K. V. K. Raju and K. Anji Reddy in Andhra Pradesh, Baba Kalyani and Habil Khorakiwala in Maharashtra, Sunil Mittal and Analjit Singh in Delhi, entered the ranks of India's billionaires at the turn of the century.

PV witnessed the emergence of new business groups from his home state of Andhra Pradesh. One of the architects of the state's industrial development was Chief Minister Jalagam Vengala Rao, also from the Telangana region, who had been PV's colleague in Indira Gandhi's government of 1980-84. PV was acutely aware of the fact that the resistance to his policies came from traditional big business groups, dubbed the 'Bombay Club' by the media. The support came from new and upwardly mobile business groups.

The story of Nagarjuna Fertilizers in Kakinada, Andhra Pradesh, is illustrative of the kind of change that industrial delicensing brought about. In the early 1980s, Andhra entrepreneur K. V. K. Raju, a former executive of Union Carbide India, decided to build a fertilizers and chemicals plant at Kakinada. His application for an industrial licence had to compete with one from the Birlas. Raju assumed that the Birlas would have contacts in New Delhi's Udyog Bhavan, home of the Ministry of Industries where licences were filed and approved. Raju was advised to tie up with an Italian company, Snamprogetti, represented in India by Ottavio Quattrocchi, because of the latter's clout in the Delhi durbar. Quattrocchi, who attained national prominence during the Bofors gun acquisition scandal in the late 1980s, was known to be influential in Delhi due to his friendship with Rajiv Gandhi's family and friends. Raju managed to secure the licence. After 1991, entrepreneurs like Raju would not have to worry about the business and political influence of big business groups like the Birlas or seek out friends of the Delhi durbar like Quattrocchi.

In 1990, the *Economic Times,* the country's most widely circulated financial newspaper, was published only out of the four metros. Readers in cities like Hyderabad and Bangalore had to wait till lunch for the Bombay edition to arrive. The publishers of the daily believed at the time that neither the readership size nor advertising revenue warranted investment in local editions in these cities. By 1995, Bangalore and Hyderabad had their own editions.

The roots of many new business families go deep into regions of India that had prospered thanks to the Green Revolution. This was how industrial capitalism developed in Europe—by rich farmers entering urban business and agrarian prosperity providing the home market for manufactured goods. In Andhra Pradesh, the TDP had emerged with the support of first generation business leaders like Ramoji Rao, Ramalinga Raju, Anji Reddy, K. V. K. Raju and so on. In Maharashtra, it was the sugarcane farmers and sugar millers who funded local political leaders even as Bombay's traditional billionaires—the Tatas and Birlas—continued to fund the Congress. In western Uttar Pradesh, a new class of rich peasants funded politicians like Charan Singh and his son, the US-returned Ajit Singh.

Seen this way, the policy unshackling of 1991 was waiting

to happen as modern capitalism took root in a feudal society transformed by agrarian change and urbanization. Surely this change impacted entrenched business interests as much as it did domestic politics. Reacting to their loss of market clout and political influence, some of India's traditional business groups—the 'Bombay Club'—met in Bombay in 1993 to consider ways in which they could manage change. Their principal concern was the takeover of Indian-owned businesses by foreign multinationals. But even as these traditional business groups sought to mobilize support from within the Congress, from traditional Congress bosses like Arjun Singh and R. K. Dhawan, the emergence of new centres of business and of new regional political parties created countervailing power that enabled PV and his reformers to transform Indian society, especially the economy and polity.

It is this new political economy and the changing geography of capitalist development that played an increasingly important role in defining the contours of economic policy in the years since. Whatever PV's critics in the Congress and Parliament may have said in 1991, the fact is that not one of his policy initiatives, taken between 1991 and 1996, was ever rolled back.

Between the United Front governments of 1996-98, the BJP-led coalition of 1998-2004 and the Congress-led coalition of 2004-14, every single major national party has either been in government or lent its support from outside to the parties in government. None of them, not one, ever sought to reverse any of PV's policies.

The debate about whether the policy initiatives of 1991 were home-grown or imposed from the outside is, therefore, meaningless. Right or wrong, they have had the endorsement of the widest cross section of democratic opinion in India.

Chapter 6

November: The Party

Most of us think of 1991 as a turning point for the economy. It should be clear now that it was also a turning point for national politics. After the long reign of the Nehru-Gandhi family from 1947 to 1989, with a three-year interruption from 1977-80, the Congress was elected to office for the first time in 1991 under the leadership of a 'non-family' political leader. Lal Bahadur Shastri, also unrelated to the Nehru-Gandhis, was prime minister in 1964-66 but he did not lead the party through an election campaign. Before he could complete the term that Nehru had won in 1962, Shastri died. He was replaced by Indira Gandhi. A member of the Nehru-Gandhi family had led the Congress to victory or defeat in every single general election since Independence.

As we have already noted, if Rajiv Gandhi had not been assassinated, the Congress would have secured fewer seats in the Lok Sabha in 1991 than it did in 1989. It was the BJP that was on the upswing. Rajiv's death triggered a sympathy wave in favour of the Congress in the second phase of the elections, but even this was mainly in the southern and western states. The BJP managed to gain ground in the north and increased its total tally in the Lok Sabha from 85 MPs in 1989 to 120 MPs in 1991.

In Andhra Pradesh, PV's home state, the sympathy wave might have combined with pride in the fact that a Telugu politician was now president of the Congress Party and could well become prime minister. N.T. Rama Rao's TDP had performed impressively in the first phase of polling on 20 May, winning 13 of the 17 seats polled, but was virtually wiped out in the second phase in June, winning only 4 of the 24 seats. Quite understandably, therefore, Rama Rao chose not to field a candidate against PV when the prime minister chose to contest from Nandyal in the Rayalaseema region of Andhra Pradesh a few months later. His election, on 17 November 1991, was near unanimous.

PV made history when his election saw the highest ever voter turnout in any democracy till that date. PV was elected with 89.5 per cent of Nandyal's voters turning up and voting for him. This was the highest voter turnout in Indian elections and earned him a place in the Guinness Book of World Records.

The victory was a morale booster for the prime minister. In 1984 and 1989 PV had had to contest from Ramtek in Maharashtra because the party was not sure if he would win in his home state against the wave of support for Rama Rao's TDP. As has been noted, in the May 1991 elections, Rajiv Gandhi had declined to give PV a party ticket, forcing him to go into political retirement. By November he was a local hero.

While PV's impressive victory in the November election helped stabilize the minority government, it appeared as if the BJP, the main opposition party, chose to support PV through his first year in office when the focus was on getting to grips with the economic situation. PV had advised his finance minister to keep opposition leaders, especially BJP leaders, informed about their policy moves.

PV's first major political move was to convene a session of the AICC in April 1992. He announced that the party would conduct organizational elections in late 1991–early 1992, ahead of the session. It had been a long time—almost two decades—since the Congress had conducted organizational elections. The last time that India's oldest and largest political party had internal organizational elections was in 1973. For two decades after that Indira and her sons, first Sanjay and then Rajiv, ran the party as if it were a family proprietorship.

The Tirupati session was historic because it was the first such session after 1966 when neither the prime minister nor the party president belonged to the Nehru-Gandhi family. In 1966, the prime minister was Lal Bahadur Shastri and the party president was K. Kamaraj. PV wanted the Congress to return to a pre-1966 trajectory, seeking a future independent of any one family. Why should the Congress remain only the 'Indira Congress'? It ought to return to its roots as the Indian National Congress, a normal political party where any member could aspire to rise to the top.

By calling for elections to party posts, including the all-powerful CWC, PV was seeking to break the power structure he had inherited, and create a new one. PV's decision to convene an AICC session also ended all talk of 'one man-one post'—that the same person should not hold both the posts of prime minister and party president. From 1980, as we have seen, the party president and prime minister were the same person—Indira and Rajiv. PV's rivals—mainly Arjun Singh and Sonia loyalists like Fotedar—demanded that PV should step down as president of the party now that he was prime minister. Rather than reject their demand, PV called for party elections that would determine who would be elected to the party's decision-making bodies. If the prime minister were to be 'elected' president, so be it.

Some commentators have suggested that PV chose Tirupati as the venue both because it was situated in the Rayalaseema region, home to his constituency of Nandyal, and also because of its religious significance as among the holiest of Hindu temples in southern India. However, there could well have been a third and a very political reason for the choice of Tirupati.

It was here that a group of five senior Congress leaders— K. Kamaraj, N. Sanjiva Reddy, Atulya Ghosh, S. Nijalingappa and Srinivas Mallya—had met in October 1963 to contemplate life after Nehru. With Nehru's health deteriorating after India's ignominious pushback by China in the border war of 1962, the big political question in India was 'After Nehru Who?' This group later evolved into what has been called 'the Syndicate' within the Congress Party. In 1991 PV may well have wanted the party to contemplate life after the Nehru family.

In a perceptive analysis of the significance of the session for the party and the prime minister, published on the eve of the session, the highly regarded political journalist K. K. Katyal observed in *The Hindu*, 'In the organizational elections that were completed recently, the party reaffirmed its faith in his [PV's] continued stewardship. This week's session will make a big demonstrative show of renewing the mandate to him, supporting his policies— economic and foreign—and approving his political line.'

PV's election as prime minister had created new hope for India's oldest political party. In it was embedded the seed of the Congress's renewal as a normal democratic political party, in which leadership is not inherited but attained through political initiative, effort and relevance. While the Tirupati session took place only in

1992, the roots of the events and outcomes there were nourished by the newly-turned soil and the monsoon of 1991.

With Rajiv's death and PV's election, the Congress became implicitly divided into four camps: First, the Nehru-Gandhi family loyalists whose power and privilege derived from their service to Rajiv and Sonia. They were the ones who had earlier made sure that Rajiv became prime minister after Indira's death and they were the most insistent on making Sonia party president after Rajiv's death. While the formal resolution inviting Sonia to lead the party was moved by PV, among others, the move was pushed by members of the coterie, including Fotedar, Dhawan and the like; second, a north Indian group led by Arjun Singh, Jagannath Mishra, and N. D. Tiwari; third, a group led by Sharad Pawar; and, fourth, a south Indian group that backed PV, actively managed by K. Karunakaran, that seemed to have the backing of the then president, R. Venkataraman.

All these groups found their individual expression in the run-up to and at the Tirupati AICC session. While PV's bête noire Arjun Singh was made convenor of the resolutions Drafting Committee, PV loyalist Jitendra Prasada, a Brahmin from Uttar Pradesh, was made convenor of the Steering Committee, organizing the session. Senior leaders representing different regions and castes found representation on the two committees. Over 400 Congress members filed nominations to contest for a seat on the all-powerful CWC. Arjun Singh demonstrated his political strength by emerging as the top scorer in the CWC elections. The other nine to get elected included, in order of votes polled: A. K. Antony, Jitendra Prasada, Sharad Pawar, R. K. Dhawan, Ghulam Nabi Azad, Balram Jakhar, Rajesh Pilot, Ahmed Patel and K. Vijayabhaskara Reddy. Pranab Mukherjee was among the losers.

Political analysts and commentators hailed the return of democracy to a family- and coterie-dominated party. In a series of perceptive comments on contemporary politics in the columns of the *Financial Express*, political scientist C. P. Bhambri of the Jawaharlal Nehru University wrote at length about these regional groupings within the Congress and the party's struggle to emerge out of the shadow of tall and strong leaders like Nehru and Indira, and become a normal political party with an elected leadership.

Things did not, however, go the way PV may have hoped, given that his arch rival emerged as the biggest scorer and his allies, Karunakaran and Mukherjee, lost while his critics, Antony and Jakhar, won. The Kautilyan PV found a way out. He expressed displeasure that not a single woman or Dalit leader had been elected. He wondered how fair the election process was. His supporters claimed that upper castes had seized the election process. PV struck quickly by suggesting that all elected members resign so that he could bring in women and Dalit representatives. In reconstituting the CWC through nominations PV brought in his friend Karunakaran, a Dalit from Maharashtra, Sushil Kumar Shinde, and Oman Deori, a tribal woman from the Northeast. He renominated all the elected members and thereby made Arjun Singh's and Pawar's tenure in the CWC subject to his authority. PV's supporters approved of this. They made the point that women, Dalit and tribal members of the party would have been unhappy that these regional satraps had sidelined weaker sections; PV had shown courage by taking them on and widening the social base of the CWC.

The Tirupati session strengthened PV and the party organization and, in doing so, became an important step in the direction of once again making the INC a truly national political party that was not identified with any one individual or family.

PV's election as party president at the Tirupati AICC diluted the enthusiasm of those who sought to bring Sonia into politics. This weakened the hold of the coterie of family loyalists on the party. On the other hand, it strengthened the position of regionally powerful political actors like Pawar, Karunakaran and Arjun Singh. Katyal summed up the mood in the party by the end of 1991 thus: 'The rank and file, however, is clear that Mr Narasimha Rao's stewardship has saved the Congress (I), and that a split would have been inevitable had she (Sonia) stepped into the shoes of her husband...Those who wanted the political resolution to affirm the party's faith in Mrs Sonia Gandhi merely evoked derisive laughter.'

■

All these developments were politically significant both for the country and the ruling party. For the first time in years the Congress was learning to function once again like a normal political party. It is interesting to note that in PV's semi-autobiographical work of fiction, *The Insider,* the character Chaudhury, chief minister of Afrozabad, the fictitious state in which PV's political life plays out, complains, 'Prime Ministership has now become proprietorship.' This draws attention to the fact that the top political position in the country was seen as a hereditary one. Chaudhury was a shrewd politician, the book's narrator, Anand, tells us. 'He was too shrewd not to be aware of the snakes and ladders game of politics, particularly with Indira Gandhi as the sole dispenser of both the snakes and the ladders.' Soon enough Chaudhury goes down a snake, as Indira Gandhi helps Anand climb the ladder to Afrozabad's chief ministership. The chief minister of a Congress-ruled state had been reduced to an employee appointed and dismissed at the whim of an all-powerful prime minister.

Within the Congress Party two theories explained the dawn of the 'era of nominated chief ministers', Anand tells us. First, that Indira Gandhi had an 'insatiable thirst for absolute power' and 'would not tolerate anyone whose political standing predated her accession to Prime Ministership'. A second, and as Anand notes, 'equally plausible' theory was that Indira Gandhi nominated chief ministers in order to 'break the stranglehold of powerful regional bosses'.

The book was a work of fiction. But all PV's observations, articulated through the various protagonists in the story, were his way of commenting on his own party. Within a decade of assuming power, Indira Gandhi changed the INC beyond recognition. In 1951, the INC was given the election symbol of two bullocks carrying a yoke. When the party split in 1967, the breakaway group that Indira Gandhi headed, called the Indian National Congress (Requisition)—INC (R)—because a group of Indira supporters 'requisitioned' a meeting at which the split with the original 'organization'—INC (O)—was made official, was given the symbol of 'cow and calf'. Few at the time made much of the fact that the cow and calf symbol represented the implicit hereditary succession in Congress leadership, from Nehru to Indira. Indeed, even fewer would have noted that this was equally a sign of things to come.

The principle of hereditary succession had not yet come to define Indian politics, though by allowing Indira Gandhi to become party president at the height of his powers, in 1959, Nehru could be accused of nepotism. At that time no other political party was headed by the offspring of a former party president who also happened to be head of government. As late as in 1966, Indira Gandhi was the only second-generation leader to step into a parent's political office, albeit with a lag.

It is possible to suggest that the first step towards inherited political power came when Motilal Nehru urged Mahatma Gandhi to name his son Jawaharlal as Congress president. Motilal did that on more than one occasion and Gandhiji obliged, to the dismay of both Subhas Chandra Bose and Vallabhbhai Patel. While Bose rejected Gandhiji's preference for Nehru, Patel was too much of a loyalist to question the Mahatma. The Mahatma's grandson, Rajmohan Gandhi, a distinguished scholar in his own right, records in his book on the Mahatma, *The Good Boatman,* 'Presiding at Lahore, Jawaharlal declared that he was "a republican and no believer in kings and princes", but the succession from father (Motilal) to son seemed to send Jawaharlal's mother Swaruprani into "a sort of ecstasy", and there were admiring references to "a king passing on the scepter of the throne to his logical successor". Gandhi, champion of the rights of the halt and the lame, the last and the least, had unwittingly launched a dynasty.'

It is this seed of hereditary succession that grew into a full-blown tree of family rule in Indira's time. Dynastic politics took a huge leap forward in 1975 when Indira Gandhi brought her son Sanjay into the decision-making circle of her party. In 1980, Indira Gandhi returned to power as though she had a divine right to rule India. The durbar that had come into being during the Emergency and remained loyal to her after she was ousted in 1977 reinforced the image that she was the natural leader of government. Without inhibition she elevated her son Sanjay Gandhi to the status of heir apparent. Those who resented Sanjay's bossism within the party and government were sidelined. A new generation of brash, young, socially upwardly mobile wannabes including Akbar Ahmed, Gundu Rao, Rukhsana Sultana, Jagdish Tytler, Kamal Nath, Ambika Soni, Bansi Lal and so on, acquired prominence both in party and government.

No other national or even major regional political leader had till then so inducted a family member into politics and policymaking. Ideology-based parties of the political Left and Right were never touched by this syndrome. The elevation of Sanjay Gandhi to a position of unquestioned power heralded a new phase of politics in India wherein a political party leader's family became the core of the party's power structure. Following this precedent, most regional and caste- or community-based political parties have adopted dynastic succession as the method of leadership transition.

Not surprisingly, therefore, when Sanjay died in a plane crash in June 1980 the coterie around Indira who ran party affairs ensured that Rajiv Gandhi, then an Indian Airlines pilot, was inducted into the party's leadership. Rajiv's induction after Sanjay's death happened as if it was the natural order of things. Fotedar offers us a ringside view of the process.

> The induction of Rajivji into politics under the mantle of the Congress Party, his careful orientation in party matters, the process of senior leaders getting accustomed to his participation in party discussions and handling of political issues—all this had taken the better part of a year since September-October 1980... [L]ater, the essential mechanics and stages of Rajivji's induction were planned and worked out. And eventually... he was in a position to file his nomination papers for the bye-election from Amethi and

after getting elected, to take his seat in the Lok Sabha as MP and in the Congress party as the *heir apparent* to the party president. (italics added)

The principle of dynastic succession, sanctified by these decisions, ensured the smooth elevation of Rajiv Gandhi as prime minister after his mother's assassination in 1984.

We now know that those in the Indira Congress who were even suspected of questioning this principle (like Pranab Mukherjee), had to pay a political price.

Long before Indira's assassination Mukherjee did come to see himself as the second-in-command in her government. I. G. Patel has a delightful story on this in his memoirs. On the eve of his stepping down as RBI governor in 1982, IG had gone to call on Indira Gandhi. After their meeting he drove down to North Block with Finance Minister Pranab Mukherjee who was also present at the meeting. As they drove out together in Mukherjee's car, the finance minister told Patel that he was then 'closest to Mrs Gandhi as she had asked him to preside at Cabinet meetings in her absence'. Adds Patel, 'I knew that if Mrs Gandhi came to know of what her finance minister was thinking—and she had a way of knowing such things—that would be the end of the Minister's dreams.' The 'dream' IG was referring to, Mukherjee's later protestations notwithstanding, was of being promoted to the top job if and when it fell vacant.

If Mukherjee had assumed that being the 'second-in-command' entitled him to step into the prime minister's shoes, he could not be faulted. The precedent was set by Gulzarilal Nanda, who was sworn in as prime minister when Nehru and Lal Bahadur Shastri died. So, when Indira died, Mukherjee would have been entitled to imagine that he could at least be an interim prime minister, like Nanda. In his teaser of an autobiography, Fotedar tells us that after Sanjay's death Indira spoke to him about potential successors to her office and mentioned the names of Mukherjee, Venkataraman and Narasimha Rao. Family loyalist that he was, Fotedar told Indira that none of the three would make the cut. He claims he suggested she draft Rajiv Gandhi. Not surprisingly, the suggestion was readily accepted. As I have mentioned earlier, it is of some significance that when Rajiv Gandhi did finally become prime minister, he chose not to include Mukherjee in his council of ministers, while retaining most of Indira Gandhi's ministers.

This era of the 'Nehru-Gandhis' came to an abrupt end in the summer of 1991. Not only had direct family rule come to an end, but even one-party dominance took a long break. Little would the members of the coterie around Sonia have imagined in the summer of 1991 that a low-profile politician like PV would have been able to demonstrate to the average member of the Congress Party that a provincial Congressman could run a Congress government as well, if not better, than a member of the Nehru-Gandhi family. PV may have had the 'charisma of a fish', as Jairam Ramesh put it, but he proved to be a better head of government than Rajiv, in terms of his ability to provide leadership at a particularly difficult period in contemporary history.

In his biography of PV, Vinay Sitapati sums it up well when he concludes: 'Prime Minister Narasimha Rao's genius in tackling these enemies of change was that he had learnt to assess political strength and weakness—his own, his opponents', and of India itself. The fact that Rao had informally accepted monkhood just two months before becoming PM shows the mental distance from power he had developed. It gave him an even clearer assessment of its constraints as well as opportunities.'

When the Congress lost the elections in 1996, PV had hoped a Congress-led coalition could still be formed. After all, even Rajiv Gandhi had considered the idea of a Congress-led coalition in 1990 before he stepped back and allowed Chandra Shekhar to form the government. PV had sent out feelers to leaders of regional parties to explore the idea of a coalition. Before he could muster support, Congressmen close to Sonia Gandhi spoke to the media conceding defeat and declared that the party would sit on Opposition benches. Two years later the party leadership reverted to the Nehru–Gandhi family.

■

For the first time after the Nehru–Gandhi family had appropriated the INC and privatized it, converting the party of India's national movement into a family proprietorship, the period of 1991-96 showed that the Congress could be repossessed by ordinary Congress persons. No one better represented that 'ordinary party worker' than PV. Making his way up the party ladder, albeit through his unquestioned loyalty to the Nehru–Gandhis, he had come to head the party's government through the normal process of selection by elected Members of Parliament. Having reached the top of the party hierarchy and government on his own merit, and not as an inheritor of a proprietorship, he chose to rejuvenate the party's democratic processes and brought back democracy within the party. This revitalization of the party cadre and provincial leadership, thanks to the organization of party elections ahead of the Tirupati session of the AICC, gave the grand old party a new lease of life. After 1991 Congress chief ministers were no longer nominated. In state after state, locally influential and powerful Congress leaders began displacing Delhi's puppets.

Before PV at least four senior political leaders—three of them ex-Congressmen—tried leading non-Congress governments in New Delhi: Morarji Desai, Charan Singh, V. P. Singh and Chandra Shekhar. All of them failed. Most of them were in office for less than a year. PV, however, demonstrated his staying power within a year. He did this not by becoming authoritarian, but by being democratic in his instincts, consensual in his approach and, above all, transactional in his dealings. His style of slow decision-making and not revealing his mind often frustrated people. But, over time, it became a new principle of political management—not taking a decision is also a decision.

Within the span of a year PV showed that the Indian economy and polity could dream of normal times, of better times; that India would enter the twenty-first century as an open society, an open economy and a normal democratic polity. India was no banana republic in which one family would rule. India was not a closed economy in which bureaucratic socialism would crush free enterprise. India could now aspire to be like many other democracies—a nation built on meritocracy and individual enterprise in which feudal privilege would no longer give anyone an advantage at birth.

The appeal of the 1991 economic liberalization for India's upwardly mobile middle classes was as much on account of the new economic opportunities that it opened up as for the new political opportunities that seemed to open up. No one understood this better than the bunch of regional political leaders who had cropped up during the 1980s across India. Stifled by the high command culture of the Indira-Rajiv Congress, many of them joined new political formations. The rise of regional parties and regional business went hand in hand. In short, 1991 became the year of new possibilities both on the economic front and the political.

In 1996, India returned to the 'era of coalitions'. After three unstable coalitions from 1996 to 1999 a stable coalition was finally constituted under the leadership of Atal Bihari Vajpayee. In 2004, another stable coalition formed a minority government under the leadership of Manmohan Singh. In between, the Congress leadership reverted to the Nehru-Gandhis with PV's successor as party president, Sitaram Kesri, yielding space to Rajiv's widow Sonia, who then took charge as party president.

In 1998, when Prime Minister Atal Bihari Vajpayee was unseated by a vote of no-confidence, Sonia made an abortive bid to become prime minister. She was thwarted by Mulayam Singh Yadav who withdrew support to the Congress-led government after indicating an initial willingness to offer it.

In May 2004, when the Congress was once again in a position to form a minority government leading a coalition, the family coterie pushed for Sonia to become prime minister. This time she wisely chose not to. However, the party adopted a new methodology to select its prime minister. It elected Sonia as the chairperson of the CPP. Sonia was then authorized to 'nominate' the head of government.

The practice till then, and in all parliamentary democracies, was that the leader of the party's parliamentary party became the head of government. In May 2004, the Congress had Sonia as chairperson of the parliamentary party, Pranab Mukherjee as leader of the party in the Lok Sabha, and Manmohan Singh as the leader in the Rajya Sabha. Sonia then nominated Singh as the party's choice to head the government. Thus, Manmohan Singh became the first nominated, rather than elected, prime minister.

It was only in May 2014 that once again a single party with a simple majority was able to form the government. This time it was a government of the BJP, headed by Narendra Modi. The Congress, led by Sonia Gandhi and her son Rahul, experienced its worst ever rout in history, securing 44 seats in the 543-member Lok Sabha.

During the intervening years the Congress Party disowned PV. His name was virtually erased from the party's public memory. When he died, the party shut the gates of its headquarters and refused to bid official farewell to a former president. His crime: seeking to end the proprietary control of the INC by the Nehru-Gandhi family. PV died on 23 December 2004. In the decade since then the only Congress leader who has regularly and religiously paid tribute and honoured PV's memory on the occasion of his birth anniversary has been Manmohan Singh—the man whose political career was made by PV. But even Manmohan Singh was unable to honour PV with a Bharat Ratna during his decade-long tenure as prime minister. The party had again become a proprietorship.

Chapter 7

December: The World

On 26 December 1991 the Union of Soviet Socialist Republics (USSR), popularly referred to as the Soviet Union, formally dissolved itself. It was the end of a historic era that began on 7 November 1917, when communist partisans, the Bolsheviks, grabbed power in Russia and ended the reign of the Tsars.

More than a year before that, in 1990, I found myself in Calcutta's Writers' Building, in the office of the only communist leader in the world who had been repeatedly elected to power in genuinely democratic elections and now in his third term in office—the redoubtable Jyoti Basu. I had gone to meet Sujit Poddar, secretary to the chief minister of West Bengal. We talked about Bengal and the world and about what was happening in the Soviet Union. The world, as the communists had known it for the greater part of the twentieth century, was changing at a dazzling pace.

Indian communists were sharply divided in their understanding of events in the communist states of Europe and Asia. The CPI (M), of which Jyoti Basu was a senior leader, had been very critical of the general secretary of the Communist Party of the Soviet Union,

Mikhail Gorbachev. I felt Gorbachev had few options left. His policy of perestroika—economic reform and restructuring—and glasnost—political liberalization—were the need of the hour. I wondered what Jyoti Basu thought of Gorbachev and his initiatives.

'Would you like to ask him?' enquired Sujit. I was not prepared for that. Would Comrade Basu have the time? That too to answer my questions? Indeed, would he be willing to?

Sujit promptly got up, went through a door that linked his room to that of his boss and returned within a minute. 'He will see you. He has some free time.'

After my initial words of introduction and respectful greetings, I popped the question. What did Comrade Basu think of Gorbachev, perestroika and glasnost?

'He is trying his best to manage the situation and take his country forward,' Basu said matter of factly. 'The Soviet Union has many problems. It is not easy. But he is trying.'

That was a sympathetic view of Gorbachev. More in line with the thinking of communists like Mohit Sen, who were admonished as 'revisionists', but certainly not in line with the CPI(M)'s official party view.

'Yes, the party does not agree with me,' Basu confessed without hesitation.

The great battles of the first half of the twentieth century were between colonialism and national liberation movements; and, between socialism and democracy, on the one side, and fascism on the other. Colonialism and fascism were defeated. In the second half of the twentieth century the battle of ideas was between bourgeois democracy and state socialism under communist party rule. The communists were on the side of the victors in the first two battles. Indeed, the communists had defeated the fascists.

But, by the end of the twentieth century, old style communist parties were losing to the appeal of Western style democracy. India was unique in that it was the only country in the world where, in a couple of states, a traditional Leninist Communist party had acquired power through parliamentary democracy. The communists in Bengal had something to teach their comrades in Europe and Asia: how to hold power through democratic elections.

'Comrade Gorbachev understands this. He is trying to combine socialism with democracy,' Basu said.

Why then did he not say any of this publicly? Why did his party continue to criticize and admonish Gorbachev? I asked.

It is not easy for people brought up with one view of the world to suddenly accept a diametrically opposite view, Basu explained. The party needed serious thinking on these issues, but there were not too many in it willing to rethink their assumptions.

To be fair, it was not just the Indian communists, constrained by their ideological straitjackets, who were unable to gauge the extent of change underway in Europe and Asia. It was not just Left ideologues who were misreading the course of history and the turn it was taking. India's diplomats, whose view of the world was shaped by the Cold War, also misjudged the mood in Moscow and across the Soviet Union.

Stuck in their diplomatic comfort zone ever since Moscow and Delhi signed a Treaty of Friendship and Cooperation in August 1971; enjoying the benefits of a rupee-rouble bilateral trade arrangement; and corrupted by the benefits of KGB largesse, India's political and diplomatic leaders were slow to grasp the nature of change underway in the Soviet Union.

True, Charan Singh and Indira Gandhi had conveyed their misgivings about the Soviet invasion of Afghanistan in 1979, fearing its destabilizing consequences for South Asia. But, by 1983, India was hosting the Seventh Non-Aligned Summit in New Delhi where the focus of the deliberations and the resolutions was on the global 'North-South' divide with no recognition of changing 'East-West' dynamics.

Even as late as in 1989, days before the Berlin Wall fell and Erich Honecker, the communist boss of East Germany, was forced to step down, the Indian Left and India's diplomats remained sanguine about the survival of East European regimes. The leadership of Romania's communist boss Nicolae Ceauşescu was being hailed in Left journals in India the very week he was dethroned in 1989.

■

Given this self-imposed mood of denial, about the extent of change underway in the communist world, it was not surprising that in August 1991 PV too misjudged the situation in the Soviet Union and went along with the assessment of Indian diplomats in Moscow—that the Soviets would endure the latest challenge to their supremacy.

Interestingly, PV's predecessor was quicker to recognize the nature of changing global power balances. By permitting US air force planes headed from the Philippines to Iraq to refuel in India, Chandra Shekhar had taken a calculated risk. He pleased the US without upsetting the two great powers of West Asia—Saudi Arabia and Iran.

That was in early 1991. By August 1991, the world had moved on. PV's early misjudgement on the foreign policy front was to make a statement in support of the aborted intra-party coup against Gorbachev. Addressing a meeting of the Youth Congress he said the coup was a warning to all those who proceeded too fast with reform. This was viewed at once as both a word of caution to India's enthusiastic reformers and as a diplomatic faux pas, since Gorbachev survived that coup attempt.

Sure, it may well have been a warning to those who wished to press on faster with reforms, given that PV was facing stiff resistance from his party's old guard. At a time when PV was defending his cautious moves towards liberalization as treading the 'middle way', a senior colleague of his who was impatient with the slowness said to me, 'Oh, it is a muddle way!'

However, on the diplomatic front it was not as much of an embarrassment as some made it out to be. As PV's friend, Nikhil Chakravartty, the legendary editor of the left-wing publication *Mainstream,* argued at the time, 'No doubt Narasimha Rao's initial observation…created confusion and could have been interpreted with good reason as a positive gesture towards the coup regime. Yet one has to understand that in the Soviet history of the last seventy years, most of the leadership changes were brought about by some sort of coup, which were legitimised by stage-managed endorsement by the party's Central Committee. There was therefore nothing frightfully wrong if Narasimha Rao had come to believe that the coup leaders had come to stay.'

For the man of caution that PV was, he surprisingly stuck his neck out on the future of the Soviet Union. Even as late as 18 September 1991, PV reassured the Lok Sabha, speaking at length on his foreign policy, 'I am quite sure that a large country like the Soviet Union just cannot go to pieces and just disappear. It is not possible.'

India was not the only country that expected the coup to fail and the Soviets to survive. Even the United States was not sure whether Gorbachev would survive the challenge. After all, just a couple of years earlier the Chinese Communist Party survived the enormous challenge that it faced in the heart of Beijing, at Tiananmen Square. Just as communist party apparatchiks won the day against pro-democracy elements in Beijing, CIA analysts too speculated that Soviet hardliners could prevail in Moscow, reducing Gorbachev to a puppet.

In August 1991, many Soviet watchers around the world assumed Gorbachev would be history. History he became, but only a few months later and no thanks to the hardliners. It was the pro-reform Boris Yeltsin who finally unseated Gorbachev and took the last steps towards undoing the statist consequences of the Russian Revolution.

After faltering in his assessment of the Soviet Union, PV slowly came to terms with the historic shift in the global balance of power and global geopolitics. Ignoring the advice of an older generation of diplomats schooled in Nehruvian pro-Sovietism and Indira's non-alignment, PV reached out to younger diplomats like Shyam Saran, Ronen Sen and Ramu Damodaran, who took a more practical view of world affairs and Indian interests. As we have seen, the irrepressible and bright J. N. Dixit soon became his key diplomatic adviser. On 15 November 1991, Dixit took charge of the foreign office.

The stocky Dixit was by then already regarded as a high calibre diplomat. He had earlier been tasked to set up India's high commission in Bangladesh after that country's liberation in 1971. His assignments as high commissioner in Colombo and Islamabad further enhanced his reputation as a no-nonsense diplomat. He was not just a skilled practitioner of diplomacy but also a scholar who wrote extensively on foreign policy. India's strategic affairs guru, the late K. Subrahmanyam, once described him to me as one of India's best foreign secretaries. Together, PV and Dixit altered the course of foreign policy, helping India adjust to the consequences of the end of the Cold War, and construct a post-Nehruvian narrative.

For someone who began his political career in the back of beyond of Telangana's Karimnagar district, and had spent most of his time in provincial politics thinking about temple administration, school education and land reforms, PV was quick to educate himself about the world. As a polyglot who read widely he became increasingly interested in the world outside. This made PV feel at home in the foreign office and most diplomats who have worked with him even fleetingly recall the pleasure of briefing him on foreign affairs. He was well informed and always ready to learn. A former diplomat's wife recalls seeing an English-Uzbek dictionary in PV's hand when he landed in Tashkent on an official visit.

PV was foreign minister in both Indira's and Rajiv's governments in the 1980s and acquired a deep understanding of a world in transition. The new US-China friendship, the entente cordiale in Europe, the East-West détente were all changing the post-colonial world order in which Nehru's policy of non-alignment had taken shape. While Indira persisted with many Nehruvian ideas in public, she imparted a pragmatic edge to Indian foreign policy—supporting the liberation of Bangladesh, opposing the Soviet invasion of Afghanistan, reaching out to Ronald Reagan and Margaret Thatcher. In his own time PV abandoned many Indian foreign policy shibboleths, reaching out to India's neighbours, recognizing Israel and pushing for nuclear tests.

■

In the Indian subcontinent the tone for the 1980s was set by two significant developments in India's wider neighbourhood. First, the emergence of Deng Xiaoping as China's new leader. Second, the Soviet Union's invasion of Afghanistan and the joint Pakistan-US led jihadi campaign against Russia. Under Deng began the inexorable rise of China. Thanks to Soviet action and US response in Afghanistan, Islamic radicalism knocked at India's door.

Deng blew the dust off Zhou Enlai's Four Modernizations of 1963 and launched, in 1978, his own revolution for the modernization and transformation of China. The modernization of agriculture, industry, national defence and science and technology were Deng's four priorities. Deng's assumption of power was preceded by a rapprochement between the People's Republic and the United States of America. This altered the Cold War balance of power across Eurasia and the Asia Pacific region. Not only had India's strategic environment been altered, but Indian attitudes towards nation-building and modernization began to change.

While the Charan Singh government conveyed India's disapproval of the Soviet action in Afghanistan, Indira Gandhi initially toned down the criticism on her return to power in 1980. However, by 1981 Indira Gandhi decided to send a different message out. The botched Soviet invasion of Afghanistan forced India to rethink its strategic relationship with the big powers.

According to Dixit, Indira sent Foreign Minister Narasimha Rao to Moscow to persuade the Soviets to withdraw from Afghanistan. Soviet Foreign Minister Andrei Gromyko called on her, asking her to 'understand' what factors led to the 'Soviet initiative', as he put it. Mrs Gandhi merely let him know that she had heard what had been said and had 'taken note of it'. She stopped short of expressing her 'understanding'.

India's own economic aspirations and woes required it to arrive at a modus vivendi with the West, especially the US. Indira Gandhi reached out tentatively to US president Ronald Reagan during his first term and Rajiv Gandhi took that initiative forward, taking advantage of a new warmth in the US-USSR relationship symbolized by the Reagan-Gorbachev dialogue. But despite tentative Indian efforts there was no qualitative change in the US-India relationship during the 1980s.

In this decade of flux, the external environment was far from comfortable for India. In many ways, India's unwillingness or inability to think its relationships anew, the rekindling of old suspicions with respect to the West, a new discomfort with an old friend, the Soviet Union, and the changing equations in Asia defined the 1980s. India retreated into an old comfort zone hosting the Non-Aligned Summit in 1983 and building new equations with other developing countries in associations such as the G-77 and G-15.

India's investment in South-South links and developing country partnerships were not particularly helpful when it came to dealing with the balance of payments crisis. In fact, in order to deal with this crisis, India's finance minister, Yashwant Sinha, had to turn to the world's rich, the Group of 7 (Canada, France, Germany, Italy, Japan, the UK and the US), for help, even if in vain. His counterpart in Tokyo did not even have time to meet him. Japan was busy doing business with China.

As that long decade came to an abrupt end, global geopolitics shifted rapidly. India was caught unawares, dealing simultaneously with political transition and economic crisis. While Chandra Shekhar was quick to grasp the implications of the fall of the Berlin Wall in 1989, Indian diplomats and strategic thinkers took time to understand what these changes in the global environment would mean for India.

By the time PV took charge the picture was clearer. Speaking to the *Economic Times* in July 1991, on the options available to the government on the economic policy front, a chastened Yashwant Sinha observed: 'The budget will mark a major departure from the kind of economic policies that have been followed since Independence. Policy will have to be viewed in the context not only of the dramatic collapse of the USSR and Eastern Europe, but also of the decisive victory of the United States in the Gulf War. The impact of these two events should not be underestimated.'

The implosion of the Soviet Union had more than geopolitical consequences for India. It also had profound economic implications at a particularly difficult time. In 1990 the Soviet Union and Eastern European countries that had rupee payment arrangement for trade with India accounted for 17 per cent of India's total external trade. This share collapsed to 2 per cent in 1992. The sharp decline in rupee trade and the Russian insistence on moving away from the rupee-rouble arrangement to hard currency payments, especially for oil, imposed a further burden on India's balance of payments. Officials in the ministries of finance and commerce were busy managing the crisis at home as well as the consequences for India of the crisis in the Soviet Union.

Political and economic change at home, a shift in the global balance of power and the geopolitical and geo-economic challenges of the day shaped India's ability to deal with the payments crisis, and the global response to it. The dramatic developments of 1991 demonstrated how the world had changed, and India with it. Professional economists have analysed in detail the economic challenges India faced at the time; political scientists and commentators have examined the political response to these challenges; and, geopolitical analysts have written extensively about shifts in global power balances. However, it is easy to see that the politics, economics and geopolitics of 1991 were all interrelated.

∎

'Now the Cold War is over, there is an element of cooperation instead of confrontation,' PV told *Sunday* magazine, in an interview in September 1991, explaining the rationale behind his economic policies. 'It is a new situation. And we have to respond to that also. So certain policy reorientation will take place to ensure that our national interest does not suffer.' In saying this, the prime minister was providing both a political rationale and geopolitical context to his domestic economic policy agenda.

In December 1991, the Chinese Premier Li Peng visited New Delhi. A new phase in India-China relations was quietly inaugurated and resulted, in 1993, in the two Asian neighbours who had fought a war along their border in 1962 signing the historic Agreement on the Maintenance of Peace and Tranquility along the Line of Actual Control in the India-China Border Areas. Whatever the continuing tensions between India and China over the years, this agreement ensured that no more lives were lost along the border in the subsequent quarter century.

∎

The impact of the new turn in economic policy and India's global economic reintegration on her diplomacy is clearly brought out by the contrasting remarks of two distinguished foreign ministers.

In an interview to the *Times of India* given in 1993, the diplomat Natwar Singh remarked: 'In my 31 years of service I never once spoke on economic issues. We thought it was infra dig to do so and left it to our commercial officers.'

On the other hand, in the same news report, the foreign minister of the day, Dinesh Singh, was quoted as saying: 'The work is cut out for our missions abroad. They will not only act as sales offices for marketing India's new economic environment but will also be responsible for communicating the feedback from the local government and business community. Above all, they should actively seek foreign investment and new markets for India's exports.'

The export push that followed the balance of payments crisis required India to place greater emphasis on relations with the world's rapidly growing markets of East and Southeast Asia. As foreign minister in Indira's cabinet, PV had travelled extensively around the region and was impressed by the development experience of Singapore, Malaysia, the Republic of Korea and Hong Kong. In Singapore he quickly established a warm and purposeful relationship with its premier, Goh Chok Tong, who spoke of an 'India fever' gripping the island nation.

A natural consequence of this search for markets and investment was PV's 'Look East Policy'. PV overturned India's longstanding reticence to dealing with the Association of Southeast Asian Nations (ASEAN) and actively sought closer links with its member countries. Focused on taking advantage of China's new policy of openness, Japan neglected India in the 1990s. Finance Minister Ryutaro Hashimoto, the man who had no time for Yashwant Sinha in early 1991 did visit India in late 1991 but no investment was forthcoming.

The outreach to Southeast Asia, through a 'Look East' policy and the outreach to West Asia, packaged in a new pragmatism, were shaped by the evolving Indian view that its geopolitical and geo-economic interests spanned a much wider circumference around the subcontinent than that suggested by the post-Independence geographical construct called 'South Asia'. India had already rejuvenated its ancient cultural links with Southeast Asia, and Nehru had tried to forge post-colonial political links, but it was left to PV to forge new economic ties in the context of the end of the Cold War and India's own economic opening up. India sought closer economic ties with Japan, Republic of Korea, Taiwan, member nations of ASEAN and even China.

Turning to the West, PV entered 1992 elevating the India-Israel relationship to the diplomatic level. India's economic rise required West Asia's energy resources as much as India's growing middle-class population needed the employment and business opportunities being generated in West Asia.

India had extended recognition to Israel in Nehru's time and did have consular relations. It even hosted a secret visit by General Moshe Dayan, the Israeli defence minister, in the late 1980s. But it was in January 1992 that the two countries established formal diplomatic relations. The decision about Israel had many dimensions to it. First, Israel was a potential supplier of defence equipment. With the implosion of the Soviet Union India had to diversify its sources of defence imports; in 1990, the Soviets supplied as much as 90 per cent of India's defence equipment. Attempts to diversify sources and bring in European suppliers suffered a blow on account of the Bofors controversy. Israel was a new and a good option.

Second, India wished to get out of the West Asian trap by maintaining good relations with all regional powers—Saudi Arabia, Iran, Egypt and Israel. Finally, Israel opened new doors for India in the United States. The powerful Jewish lobby in the US held the key to many doors in the corridors of power and wealth along the US East Coast. India was seeking money and a new strategic equation with the world's biggest economy and the sole superpower. Establishing diplomatic relations with Israel was one more initiative towards that end.

■

PV's first foreign tour as prime minister was, however, to Germany. He told Parliament that this decision was shaped by economic considerations. The US victory in the Cold War might have turned the world 'unipolar' in military terms, PV told the Lok Sabha in September 1991, 'but in the economic sense it is multi-polar, it is multi-centric'.

Germany lay at the heart of the new European project. The unification of the European market would create a new global economic entity led by Germany. That is why, PV explained, he chose to make Germany his first port of call.

In emphasizing the emerging global economic multi-polarity at a time when geopolitical analysts were all focused on US military power and the new 'unipolar' world that they thought would replace the dying 'bipolar' Cold War era, PV was prescient. The US had an exaggerated sense of its military power at the end of the Cold War and got embroiled in military conflicts in Eastern Europe and West Asia, while China quietly built its economic capability. Today's multi-polar world has been built on the foundations of globally dispersed economic development, especially the rise of China as an economic superpower.

European geopolitical analysts have only recently begun to view Germany as a 'geo-economic power', but PV's remarks in Parliament in 1991 suggest an early Indian appreciation of the changing nature of international relations in the post-Cold War era. To view the world as multi-polar or multi-centric, as PV did, because of the global dispersal of economic power, without being overwhelmed by the concentration of military power among a few, shows a very sophisticated strategic mind at work.

In PV's time, when the US still enjoyed overwhelming military power, only a few scholars like Samuel Huntington at Harvard, were emphasizing the importance of economic power. We now know from Sitapati's biography of PV that he was in fact familiar with Huntington's writings and may well have been aware of how historians and strategic analysts were beginning to view the nature of power in the post-Cold War world. Once the brief post-Cold War 'unipolar moment' was over, with the US-led fiasco in Iraq, the global balance of power was increasingly shaped by geo-economics. Nothing symbolized this better than China's rise as a trading superpower.

Manmohan Singh put it pithily in his budget speech of July 1991 when he spoke of 'the emergence of India as a major economic power in the world'. This, he believed, was an idea whose time had come. Power no longer lay in the barrel of the gun, but in a nation's economic capability. India's foreign policy must henceforth seek to create a global environment conducive to India's economic betterment and empowerment.

This way of thinking about countries that mattered for India also shaped India's 'Look East Policy'. PV reached out to Southeast Asian countries by building bridges with Singapore and Malaysia. He established a good personal equation with Malaysian prime minister Mahathir Mohamad and Singapore prime minister Goh Chok Tong. As India 'Looked East', Goh encouraged ASEAN to 'Look West' to India.

Even as he improved relations with ASEAN, PV became the first Indian prime minister to travel to the Republic of Korea. In Seoul, he urged Korean chaebol to invest in India in a big way. In 1991, there was no major Korean brand available in the Indian market. A decade later, Samsung and Hyundai had become household names across the subcontinent. In the months to come India would also take steps to establish closer links with Taiwan.

In sum, even as the end of the Cold War forced India to come to terms with shifts in global geopolitics, its domestic economic situation also required it to focus on the new geo-economics of globalization. Building bridges with Germany, Japan, Republic of Korea, Taiwan and the member countries of ASEAN was a natural response of a country seeking to stabilize its external economic profile, rebalance relations between major powers and accelerate the rate of growth of the economy. In the years that followed it was this thinking that defined the role of BRICS—the coalition of middle powers—Brazil, Russia, India, China and South Africa.

It was against this background that India reformulated its foreign policy by prioritizing its national economic interests. As early as in December 1947, Nehru did emphasize the primacy of economic policy in defining foreign relations when he told the Constituent Assembly, 'Talking about foreign policies, the House must remember that these are not just empty struggles on a chessboard. Behind them lie all manner of things. Ultimately foreign policy is the outcome of economic policy.'

As India's economic policies and priorities shifted, gradually in the 1980s and dramatically in 1991, so too did its strategic and foreign policy objectives. India was no longer content being viewed as a leader of the 'non-aligned movement' or of the Group of 77 developing countries. PV took an active interest in the newly-created G-15, a sub-group of the more developed and open economies among members of the Non-aligned Movement, created in 1989 to pursue trade and investment liberalization aimed at promoting their development. PV often deputed his finance minister, Manmohan Singh, to travel the world and build bridges with developed economies. As Dixit records in his comprehensive account of Indian foreign policy from 1947 to 2003, 'Narasimha Rao's stewardship of India's foreign policy in a period of volatile transitions in world affairs would be judged as adroit and successful.'

PV and Dixit left their decisive imprint on India's post-Cold War foreign policy, constructing a new post-Nehruvian paradigm that emphasized realism and privileged economic self-interest in the pursuit of international relations.

The Nehru-Indira era in foreign policy was defined by multiple imperatives: (*a*) the Cold War and a desire to remain outside the military blocs of that era; (*b*) India's quest for a global role as a post-colonial nation committed to the empowerment of other nations of the global South; and (*c*) India's own development needs. This phase began to end in the 1970s. The 1980s was a decade of flux in Indian foreign policy. On the one hand, India would host the Non-aligned Summit and propose universal nuclear disarmament, on the other, it would reach out to the West and quietly build its own nuclear capability. This incipient pragmatism of the 1980s found freer expression during PV's time and after. Indian foreign policy was increasingly defined by the demands of economic development and India's reintegration into the global economy. India needed markets, technology, capital. India wanted a quieter and more stable neighbourhood. India had to catch up on the development front with East and Southeast Asia. India needed an assured supply of energy and access to new employment opportunities for Indians in West Asia.

Each of India's important bilateral relationships, perhaps with the singular exception of Pakistan, was defined by the new economic realities of an increasingly open economy. An inward-oriented India, like all developing countries that pursued import-substituting industrialization, worried about external dependence. A more outward-oriented India, like all newly and rapidly industrializing economies of Asia, began to discover the value of building relations of inter-dependence with countries that mattered.

Chapter 8

The Middle Way

This book is about India in 1991. Its central character could well have been Chandra Shekhar. The two events that defined that year and shaped India's destiny—an economic crisis and the end of the Cold War—were well within Chandra Shekhar's grasp and he showed the capability to deal with them. If he had had the political support, he would have. He lost his place in history because he lacked the numbers in Parliament. Narasimha Rao gained that place because he not only acquired the numbers, but made sure those numbers remained securely with him, and increased with time.

Rajiv Gandhi too played an important role. He made an incipient crisis worse by withdrawing support to the Chandra Shekhar government, and not allowing it to present a reformist budget in time to secure a lifeline from the IMF. Of course, his government and others in the 1980s contributed to the crisis with their irresponsible fiscal policies. On the positive side, Rajiv helped manage the crisis even in his death by giving his imprimatur to the policies that PV eventually implemented. Rajiv did not have the political courage to do so. PV did.

Rajiv contributed to the Congress victory in 1991 with his life.

It was his dastardly assassination that gave his party the numbers to form a government. In that hour of crisis, the diminutive, retiring PV stepped up.

Much has been written about the economic crisis and the reforms of 1991. But most of that has been written by economists who regard themselves and their tribe as the key actors. Economists think of themselves as modern day prophets and saviours. Historian Robert Skidelsky titled the second volume (dealing with the inter-war crisis years) of a three-volume biography of John Maynard Keynes, the most influential economist of the twentieth century, *The Economist as Saviour*.

Keynes and his fellow economists, says Skidelsky, viewed themselves as members of an 'activist intelligentsia, claiming a right of direction, vacated by the aristocracy and the clergy, by virtue of superior intellectual ability and expert knowledge of society.' They saw themselves as 'the front line of the army of progress'.

Ever since, economists have basked in this self-image as social saviours and commanders on the development battlefront. They have also been the most successful among social scientists in cornering cushy jobs in government and international economic organizations.

Being a Cambridge student and an admirer of the Soviet Union, Jawaharlal Nehru was drawn to economic planning and to economists. He hired many and named himself chairman of a Planning Commission—an institution populated by economists. From Nehru's time to now, professional economists have been the modern day courtiers in the Delhi durbar, serving successive prime ministers, helping them build what I have often called their 'policy Taj Mahals'—public policy initiatives, schemes and projects that politicians in power wish to be remembered by.

Learning from the experience of her first tenure in office, Indira Gandhi chose to keep economists of both the Left and the Right on her side when she returned to power in 1980. She pleased the Left with her policies of the 1970s. She won over the Right by going to the IMF in 1981 and implementing a Fund-approved programme. As we have seen, the 'Indira generation' among economic policymakers, so to speak, has always claimed that the real turn in the economy's fortunes began in the late 1970s and early 1980s, while those involved in policymaking in 1991 and after would prefer to think of the 1990s as the real turning point for the economy.

After the turn of 1991, professional economists in government became divided: they were either friends of Manmohan Singh who would hail him and his contemporaries as the real revolutionaries in policymaking or left-of-centre economists from the Indira-era like Arjun Sengupta, who took a different view, claiming prior ownership of the ideas that came to define the policy shift in 1991. They would differentiate their own 1980s brand of reform from that of Singh's 1990s reform.

Part of the battle between economists was fought on the statistical front. It was all about cut-off years and when the growth curve shifted. Was the acceleration of growth in the last few years of the last century more on account of changes in policy or mainly due to an increase in productivity? Was it rural demand or growing urbanization that made the difference? Were the 1980s initiatives truly 'pro-market' or merely 'pro-business'?

Note, however, the fact that many of the economists who were in government in the 1990s were also in government in the 1980s. Why then did 1991 become a turning point for the economy? Prime Minister Narasimha Rao would be amused when told about such argumentation among economists. Whatever their individual claims about their role in policymaking, he would say, tongue-in-cheek, 'It is we politicians who appoint them. Was it not my decision to induct an economist into my team?'

A few years before PV passed away a former official of the Finance Ministry asked him how much credit he would like to take for the reforms of 1991-92, and how much credit would he give to Manmohan Singh. PV praised Singh and acknowledged his loyalty and his contribution to reforms. Then, in his characteristic deadpan manner, he said to his interlocutor, 'A finance minister is like the numeral zero. Its power depends on the number you place in front of it. The success of a finance minister depends on the support of the prime minister.'

■

By taking charge of policy in the summer of 1991, PV made history. But, as I have noted, he made sure he took no individual credit for it, claiming that what he did is what Rajiv Gandhi would have wanted to do. He told the Tirupati session of the AICC in April 1992, 'In the past ten months, our Government has initiated far-reaching fiscal and financial reforms. This was done in conformity with our Election Manifesto of 1991 which gives the main features of the reforms.'

Suggesting that there was no deviation in his policies from Nehru's vision of a 'socialist India', PV projected his initiatives as ensuring 'continuity with change'. A country of India's size 'has to be self-reliant', PV told the AICC, but self-reliance did not mean the pursuit of import substitution as a dogma. 'The very level of development we have reached has made us independent of the world economy in some respects, but more dependent on it in others.'

Self-reliance in 1991, PV believed, could be defined as being 'indebted only to the extent we have the capacity to pay'. Reducing foreign debt, being able to avoid default, promoting exports and liberalizing the economy so as to attract foreign investment and earn foreign exchange were all elements that would define the path to self-reliance. In the past, self-reliance had been defined as securing 'independence' from the world economy, now self-reliance was being redefined as creating 'inter-dependencies' that would give others a stake in India's progress.

Next, PV went on to redefine the role of the public sector, reminding his party that both the profits and the losses of public enterprises were in fact the profits and losses of the people of India. Making the public sector more efficient, so that it would cease to be loss-making, was in the interest of the people. Further elaborating the role of public and private sectors in the economy PV claimed his policies 'do not represent the withdrawal of the State altogether, but a reconsideration of the areas in which it must be present'.

Finally, PV went on to redefine yet another Nehruvian idea that had been reduced to a shibboleth by Indira Gandhi's diplomats. Non-alignment was not just about remaining outside antagonistic military alliances. It was not about being 'neutral'. Non-alignment is 'an urge for independence in judgment and action, in exercise of the sovereign equality of nations'. As a non-aligned nation India could choose a side in international relations depending on the issue. While India chose to be outside any alliance, it retained the freedom to work with one or the other alliance depending on its own national interest.

This was a pragmatic, not ideological, view of non-alignment.

After all, in 1962, Nehru was willing to seek US military help to deal with China and in 1971 Indira sought Soviet help to deal with the ganging-up of the US and China on the issue of the future of East Pakistan. The Polish economist Michał Kalecki described non-alignment as 'a clever calf sucking two cows', drawing attention to the policy's pragmatic rather than ideological basis.

Linking his economic policies to his foreign policy, PV concluded, 'This self-reliance must consist in trying to find solutions to our own problems primarily according to our own genius... We reject nothing useful for its plainness, we take nothing irrelevant for its dazzle.'

PV called it the 'middle way'. PV's 'middle way' is not to be confused with a 'middle path'. It was not a mean or a median, a compromise between extremes. It was a path unto itself. As PV told the AICC, 'To interpret Nehru's middle way as being valid only in a bi-polar situation is not to understand our ancient philosophy of the Middle Way.'

Writing a few years later, in 1998, British sociologist Anthony Giddens called it the 'third way' in his politically influential book, *The Third Way: The Renewal of Social Democracy.* It was said to have inspired the politics of Prime Minister Tony Blair who was himself battling the Right and Left within the Labour Party. Rejecting top-down bureaucratic socialism and its emphasis on public investment and controls, as well as rejecting laissez-faire 'neo-liberalism', PV's 'middle way' sought to 'strike a balance between the individual and the common good', as PV put it.

It was the best expression of a liberal principle that in a different world a very different man summed up as 'seeking truth from facts'.

■

Guiding India through new and hitherto uncharted terrain, in that fateful year, PV became the man of the moment. It is a tragedy of Indian politics that PV's leadership on the economic, foreign policy and domestic political fronts has not received the recognition it deserves. His own party let him down, on the specious plea that his inaction during the destruction of the Babri Masjid in Uttar Pradesh in December 1992 had alienated the Muslim community. That is another story altogether, and one which begins in 1985 with Rajiv Gandhi and his advisers opening the doors of the Babri Masjid to Hindus who wished to pray there.

For his part, PV is the only prime minister who has left behind an entire book explaining his side of the story on a major issue of his tenure. In PV's view, as he sums up in the book, *Ayodhya: 6 December 1992*, published posthumously, 'I tried to explain all these things to my colleagues, but on their side also political and vote-earning considerations definitely prevailed and they had already made up their minds that one person was to be made historically responsible for the tragedy, in case the issue ended up in tragedy. If there had been success (as there definitely seemed to be, in the initial months) they would of course have readily shared the credit or appropriated it to themselves.'

The real collapse of the Congress occurred in the 1980s. PV held everything together. He helped stabilize the economy and make the strategic shifts India was required to make in the post-Cold War era, recognizing the nature of the emerging multi-polar world. Of course, PV had his flaws and made his mistakes. Of course, there was much that was wrong with his government. But, in that one year, 1991, he offered quiet, sober and competent leadership to a nation unnerved by multiple crises and unforeseen changes and challenges.

From vanaprastha he was on the verge of taking up sanyasa. He was called upon to be a karmayogi. For the leadership he provided in that fateful year PV deserved the Bharat Ratna. It is a sad commentary on this nation of ours that we do not know who our real heroes are and do not know how to honour them.

The year 1991 was one of crisis and tragedy. It was also the year of new possibilities and new resolve. If India won its political independence in 1947, a new generation of Indians believed they had won their economic independence in 1991. It marked the beginning of a new phase of economic development and strategic engagement for India. It also defined new political possibilities.

Thinking about 1991 today may help us think anew on each front. It could inject new self-confidence into India's political leaders as they pursue once again 'reforms with a human face'. It could help clarify the choices we have to make as we engage a changing world.

It could also help inject confidence into a new generation of Congress supporters who may yet find the courage to imagine a different future for the Indian National Congress. For, as we have seen, 1991 was the year in which the Congress Party grabbed the opportunity to return to its origins as a national political party, and not just one more of the many family-dominated parties. Since then the 'Indira Congress' has morphed into the 'Sonia Congress'. Can the party once again claim to be the Indian National Congress, as it could at Tirupati in 1992?

Today the BJP and the Communists are among a handful of political parties that can claim that their political future is not a function of the physical longevity of their current leadership and that the emergence of a new leadership is not a function of their family and kinship ties.

PV gave a new lease of life to the Indian economy by boldly implementing policies that his predecessors may have wanted to but did not. He imparted new self-confidence to Indian diplomacy by quickly building new bilateral relationships in a fast changing world. He also gave new hope to his party members around India by showing that the Congress Party need not depend only on one family to run a successful government.

For all these reasons 1991 was a landmark year. However, for all his erudition and sense of history, PV may not have viewed 1991 in such stark terms. We write with the benefit of hindsight, and hindsight is only available in the future.

Reading the way we view 1991, PV may well have chuckled and recalled the words of historian Hobsbawm:

> Students of the process of modernization in twentieth century India have investigated the ways in which powerful and rigid traditional systems can be stretched or modified, either consciously or in practice, without being officially disrupted, that is in which innovation can be reformulated as non-innovation.

It is a measure of his modesty that in his own lifetime he never made any claims about either making history or how he would be judged by it. In that sense, he had internalized the qualities of a sanyasi.

This book is not about PV's tenure as prime minister. We have only seen a glimpse of the historic role he came to play in a landmark year. Democratic politics does not always offer an opportunity to a politician to become a statesman. Even when such an opportunity presents itself, all politicians do not have the wisdom, the resolve and the guile to acquire a statesman's sheen. PV did. He grabbed an opportunity that presented itself the day he took charge. He entered the history books within a month of entering his high office.

If he had succeeded in conducting nuclear weapon tests in the winter of 1995, as he had planned to, his tenure would not only have begun with a bang but also ended with one, so to speak. In the event, he left the opportunity to test and declare India a nuclear weapons state to his friend and successor, Atal Bihari Vajpayee.

Every head of government anywhere in the world, more so in a democracy, lives through the ups and downs of a nation's life and a government's tenure. PV too had his highs and his lows. It is a pity that his own party has chosen to remember him by his lows. Two decades after he demitted office and a decade after his passing away, India is finally coming around to remembering him by the highs of his first year in office. This book has tried to capture that story.

Acknowledgements

At two dinner meetings in Hyderabad in 2015, one hosted by Ramesh Gelli and another by Vamsi Maddipatla and members of the Entrepreneurs' Organization, I was encouraged by many of the city's business leaders and young entrepreneurs to write a book on P. V. Narasimha Rao and his role in 1991. I thank them for their interest and hope they will all like this book.

Thanks are due to Kashyap Arora for the research assistance he provided. I am grateful to Nalin Surie and the librarian at the Indian Council of World Affairs, New Delhi, for giving me access to bound volumes of the newspapers of 1990 and 1991. I should also thank Pratap Bhanu Mehta and the staff of the Centre for Policy Research for their hospitality. I am indebted to Nandini Mehta, Ritu Vajpeyi-Mohan, Pujitha Krishnan, Joydeep Mukherjee and Aseema Sinha for very helpful suggestions that have helped me improve earlier drafts of the book. I am particularly grateful to Ritu Vajpeyi-Mohan for the enthusiasm with which she has ensured the timely publication of this book.

I am deeply grateful to Ramu Damodaran, Naresh Chandra, Rakesh Mohan, Yashwant Sinha Deepak Nayyar, P. V. R. K. Prasad, I. Ramamohan Rao, Kalyani Shankar, Ronen Sen, Vinay Sitapati and V. Srinivas for sharing their thoughts about PV and his role in 1991.

Finally, a word of thanks to my father, B. P. R. Vithal, for encouraging me to write this book. He knew PV, warts and all. This book is my gift to him in his ninetieth year.

Appendix

PRESIDENTIAL ADDRESS: TIRUPATI CONGRESS PLENARY

Esteemed Chairman of the Reception Committee,
Mr. Chief Minister
Respected Party Colleagues,
Fellow Delegates,
Excellencies, Fraternal Delegates,
Friends,

1. We meet today at a holy place. May this national congregation have the benediction of the Almighty, in whatever name or form humans offer their worship to Him. This is a moment of great significance, for it is after close on two decades that the Indian National Congress is meeting in Plenary session after organisational elections. I offer my congratulations to you, accredited representatives of this great organisation. I greet all Congressmen from all over the country, gathered here in such large numbers, determined in their resolve to serve the country with faith and dedication. I extend a hearty welcome to our fraternal delegates who have graced the occasion, coming from several countries of the world. I am grateful to the Andhra Pradesh Congress Committee for having made this Plenary possible, at an incredibly short notice. Only abiding faith in the Party could have enabled them to undertake this task.

2. I cannot find adequate words to thank you for the great privilege you have bestowed upon me. The Presidentship of the Indian National Congress is a very high political honour in the country. This distinction has given me a great sense of pride and fulfilment in life.

3. Like many of you here who belong to my generation, I began in the Congress as a humble footsoldier in Mahatma Gandhi's Swaraj Yatra. Gandhiji's message was clear. It was the same as had been taught centuries earlier by the

BHAGAVAD GITA: that we have a right only to action and service and not to the fruits thereof. Our other teacher, Jawaharlal Nehru, used to say that we are small men but something of the greatness of our cause makes us great to some extent. We come and go. But our motherland is eternal, like the Ganga, the Himalayas, Kanyakumar and the Tirumalai hills. Being born in this hallowed and beloved land, it is our duty to work for it in such a way that nothing diminishes its greatness.

4. We miss one person who should have been in our midst today, directing our deliberations -- Rajiv Gandhi. At a young age he left his impress on this old land. In a very short time, he came to acquire the stature of a world leader. His daring, his dynamism, his instinctive understanding of the economic and technological forces at work in the world, and of the compulsions of a world in which political relations were changing beyond recognition, his capacity for unsparing toil and, above all, his limitless love for the people of India: all this had given us the feeling that in him the leadership of the country had been settled for at least twenty years. But that was not to be. He set out on a courageous act of good neighbourliness, but fell victim to the cruel destiny traceable to the same noble act. That is martyrdom, Rajiv Gandhi, like his mother, was a great martyr. It was a poignant inheritance from mother to son.

It is difficult to believe even today that Rajiv Gandhi is no more. The reason is simple; he is very much with us in our thoughts, in our emotions. In a month's time the first anniversary of his martyrdom is coming. We shall observe the occasion all over the country in such a way that we continue to derive inspiration from his life and work.

5.   The organisational elections have revived our party and given us a new elan. I pay my tribute to the thousands of Congressmen and Congresswomen who made them a success and the hundreds who bore the responsibility of conducting them. The elections have refuted the charge that our party had been converted into self-perpetuating power groups. Regardless of these charges, we live by our own lights. The Indian National Congress is the largest democratic party in the world; it will continue to remain so. Moreover, the Congress is the party which has the capacity to preserve India's democratic way of life and its integrity. It is the party which can promote all the values that the name India signifies -- an ancient civilisation with a genius for constant renewal, a harmonious family of many religions, many languages, many races and many tribes, each realising its full potential.

6.   Since the last Plenary in 1985, we have lost a number of prominent leaders. Babu Jagjivan Ram was also one of our former Presidents, apart from being a leader of the country in his own right. We mourn his loss. We mourn the demise of Khan Abdul Ghaffar Khan, affectionately known as "Frontier Gandhi" whom the people of this country venerated profoundly and who was one of our most prominent freedom fightier. Mrs. Vijaya Lakshmi Pandit was an unforgettable figure in the country's history. Chowdhary Charan Singh was a leader of great stature and Prime Minister for some time.

We pay respectful homage to Shri Kamlapati Tripathi, Shri Umashankar Dixit, Shri M.G. Ramachandran, Shri H.K. Mahtab, Shri Baba Prithivi Singh the doyen among freedom fighters, Shri D.P. Mishra, Shri Vasant Dada Patil, Sardar Darbara Singh, Shri H.N. Bahuguna, Shri G.S. Dhillon, Captain Williamson Sangma, Shri K.H. Patil, Shri T. Anjaiah, Shri Vir Bahadur Singh, Shri Radha Raman, Shri Shamsuddin and Shri Chandrasekhar Singh.

I am mentioning here only a few names whom we have lost and to wom we paid homage in our condolence resolution on April 14. Obviously, the list cannot be exhaustive.

I would particularly pay a special homage to all those who have become victims of terrorist violence in several parts of the country.

This state of Andhra Pradesh has played a significant role in the freedom struggle. It has witnessed some inspiring and unforgettable scenes. Imagine the great Prakasam Pantula baring his chest to the bullets of police at the time of Simon Commission. Imagine the frail but firm Swami Ramananda Tirtha bluntly telling the Nizam of Hyderabad: " I shall break but not bend." Imagine the gentle Pothi Sriramulu going on a fast-unto-death, and finally courting death with dogged determination for a separate State. Imagine hundreds of whole families, husband, wife and child, going to jail in the Satyagraha movement, even without remembering to lock their houses. Imagine thousands upon thousands Congressmen and Congresswomen marching defiantly all over the State chanting the stirring song "MakøddiuTella Dŗa Tanamu," meaning, "we don't want this white man's rule!" Imagine the large number of women donating all, repeat all their jewellery, taken out on the spot, to Mahatma Gandhi for his Harijan Fund, in a noble gesture that came to be called Niluon Dopidi (standing robbery). And finally, the scenes during the 1942 Quit India Movement which again have become immortal in the history of India.

Some of us were fortunate to have seen those items. The people here have done their bit, along with their compatriots all over the country.

7.   Since the last regular Plenary of 1972, we have gone through some radical turns. 1971 and 1972 were years of glory for the Congress, to be more exact "Indira Congress". The Party sewpt the polls, on the inspiring call of garibi hatao which Indiraji gave the nation. Those were memorable elections, moments of pride for the Congress.

.8.   It was soon clear, however, that de-stabilising forces at home and abroad would not let the Congress rest.   Jhe

country went into a trying period and a National Emergency
had to be imposed to cope with the situation. The democratic
process thus came under strain. Influenced by incessant
disinformation, the people got temporarily alienated from the
Congress. Came 1977 and the first debacle of the Congress at
the Centre and the formation of the first non-Congress
Government of the Janata Party.

9.   Within a year of the Janata Party's advent, the people
realised the truth. They discovered that they had unwittingly
ushered in a government with no cohesion, no will and no
capacity to deliver the goods. A split occurred in the Congress
at the end of 1977-- between those who followed Indira
Gandhi steadfastly and those who thought her a spent force
and deserted her. Then started the comeback of the Congress,
from here in Andhra Pradesh and neighbouring Karnataka.
Thereafter it was only a question of time. The Janata Party
Government collapsed under the weight of its own
contradictions and the Congress, under Indira Gandhi, came
back to power in 1980.

10.   Indira Gandhi's return as Prime Minister brought in
an era of stability and purposeful governance once again.
Yet, the country was not left in peace to pursue its path of
orderly progress. The Punjab and Assam problems erupted,
in a virulent form. The nation's attention was diverted to the
immediate task of fighting terrorism and secessionism.
Violence overtook many parts of the country, taking different
forms, seeking to disrupt the country's unity. Regional parties
also grew in stature and strength. Just as the country was
about to go to polls in 1984, the hand of the assassin snatched
away our leader and Prime Minister Indira Gandhi. At that
hour of our deepest grief, Rajiv Gandhi came to our rescue.
Overnight, he became the country's natural leader, supported
by a fund of goodwill and affection from the masses of India.
The forces of destabilisation were once again check-mated.

11.   Rajiv Gandhi's term as Prime Minister has been unique in several ways. It had the confidence of leadership settled for a long time to come, the freshness of youth, a perfect understanding of the emerging modern trends, the solid base of Indianness all the way and a far-sighted vision of the country's entry into the next century. But as fate would have it, his long-term vision was abruptly cut short by assassination just when he was poised to lead   the Government once again. The country has thus faced two tragedies in quick succession. The Congress has lost its two great leaders when they were required most. It is ten months since tragedy struck the country. We stand at the cross-roads of history today, in a world of bewildering complexities. The country once again looks up to the Congress for guidance, to the Indian National Congress that has never wavered in any moment of crisis, never faltered under the pressure of any adversity.

Fellow delegates, where do we go from here?

I shall set out in some detail what I see ahead of us. I shall begin with the ideological framework.

12.   For the Indian National Congress, Mahatma Gandhi is both symbol and substance. The organisation has not quite come to his level in behaviour and performance; yet he has been the sole beacon light for succeeding generations of Congressmen. And so it will be, so long as one can foresee. Indeed Gandhi is sure to become more and more relevant to the world, in its bewildered march towards a destiny as yet unclear, when the old shibboleths are crumbling one by one. There is no substitute for Truth, no alternative to Non-violence. We in the Congress, therefore, pledge to follow him, with whatever imperfections such a huge party could be heir to, from time to time. We shall strive to imbibe his simplicity, his steadfastness, his firmness, his concern for the down-trodden, and above all, his readiness to admit mistakes

and learn from them.   We shall
attempt to return to his Gram Swaraj and to implement a
version of his constructive programme for the socio-economic
amelioration of the poorest, the *daridranarayana* who was the
focus of his attention. We shall cut ostentation and eradicate
corruption and vulgarity. I could do no better than begin with
this PLEDGE.

13.   The four pillars of the Indian polity -- democracy,
secularism, socialism and Non-alignment -- will always be
our ideological sentinels. We shall always cherish and
nourish them. Nothing will ever make us deviate from these
hallowed paths. We shall never allow our faith in these to get
dimmed.

        I shall now deal with each of these components of our
ideology separately: .

14.   From what I have just said on the fluctuating electoral
fortunes of political parties, one indelible fact stands out:
Democracy has come to stay in India; the Indian electorate has
excelled itself in maturity and wisdom. They have tried
several parties, giving them a fair chance to prove their worth.
They have often blessed the Congress, but on occasions
rejected it unhesitatingly and unceremoniously.   The
Congress, each time, bowed to their verdict and continued to
serve them, regardless of victory or defeat. It has proved
conclusively that it is *of the people*, while names and styles
have changed with each election in the case of some other parties.

15.   The Congress reaffirms its unchanging commitment to
secularism. This is the very essence of the Congress vision.
This has always been our faith, our ethos. We believe that in
India there can be no democracy without secularism. Indeed
there can be no India without secularism. Democracy here
means secular democracy, pure and simple. People of all

communities, faiths and persuasions have equal rights in our polity. We oppose communal and caste issues being brought into the political process for electoral gains; such issues just do not belong in this process. Our fight in the defence of secularism has been relentless; it will always remain so. Protection to minorities will always remain an article of faith with us.

16. At this point, I would like to raise a basic question for the consideration of the political parties and the people of this country. Under Indira Gandhi, the Parliament made a basic and well-considered Amendment in the Indian Constitution. The fact that this was brought about two and a half decades after the Constitution came into force, is significant. It means that much serious thought went into its making. It is high time that the full implications of this Amendment are realised for further action.

17. As per this Amendment, India was declared a *secular* State. Despite some cynical comment at the time and thereafter, I submit that this Amendment was extremely important. It was neither meant as a mere assertion of the existing situation, nor as a publicity device. It was intended for serious consideration and action.

18. The Constitution has since defined a political party in the Anti-defection law of 1985. This opens up a great opportunity for the Indian polity. It is only logical to expect that a secular democracy should be run with the participation of secular political parties. Non-secular parties should have no place in the conduct of a secular democratic State. Any electoral contest between secular and non-secular parties clearly goes against the spirit of the above Amendment of the Constitution. Besides, such a contest is neither fair nor healthy. It often involves, in some way or another, an overlay of non-secular propensities on the secular consciousness of the electorate. Any election in which an issue tends to range

one community against another, is an anti-thesis of secular democracy. There could indeed be disputes between communities, castes etc., but seeking to resolve them through an election cannot be in the spirit of the Constitution. Surely there should be other methods of resolving such issues. I do not think this requires much argument.

19.   The question, however, is how to define a secular party and to determine recognisable criteria to distinguish between a secular political party and a non-secular party. A detailed public debate is necessary on all aspects of this issue. It would be entirely reasonable to say that a political party that participates in the secular democratic process must present a secular face, and a secular choice, to the electorate. I would therefore urge upon the leaders of public opinion to appreciate the desirability of ensuring the truly secular character of the democratic process in all respects, in the spirit of the Constitution. This, I am sure, will prove beneficial to our secular democracy.

20.   Returning to ideology, we saw another ideology loom large on the world scene during the greater part of this century. As a political party, we have to analyse that development dispassionately and draw the right lessons from the collapse of that ideology. Nothing can change the fact that when the Russian Revolution first occurred in 1917, it had an impact. It affected global events directly and influenced the thinking of several leaders of the world. Jawaharlal Nehru took note of it and realised its potential and implications, although he remained essentially anchored in the Gandhian thought, in the Indian context. The period between the two World Wars witnessed the increased aspirations of colonial countries for their liberation. It also widened their political vision, inasmuch as their struggle for political freedom became a means to achieve economic freedom. As a result, the world was re-polarised after the Second World War and not

merely re-adjusted between imperialist powers, as had happened in the wake of earlier wars.

21.   Any society must answer the question: "How much to collect from each and how much to give to each." The first has a bearing on production and the second on distribution. Every society also has to fulfil its needs. But then the further questions also arise: Whose needs? What needs? In any just society with limited resources, the needs of a few cannot get primacy over the needs of many or all. Again, since there are needs and needs, one has to categorise some of them as basic needs and accord priority to them.

22.   Mankind is also realising more and more today that the catalogue of needs cannot be infinite. Likewise, the capacity to satisfy those needs cannot be unlimited. This bitter truth has brought about a big change in man's thinking, because of the limited resources of this planet. Gandhiji pleaded that we cannot build our society on the basis of a continuous increase of human needs and their satisfaction. Today, we can clearly see that this far-sighted perception is based not on a moral premise alone, but on the hard realities of physical constraint. Given a constraint of this nature, we must always give priority to the satisfaction of the common needs of the largest number. Other needs, which consume more resources, which only some sections of the people can afford, get comparatively lower priority for the moment. This is the modern relevance of the Gandhian approach. The content of our new socialistic approach will have to be in these choices. And the process has to be democratic.

23.   We have, however, constantly to find new ways to retain the original vigour of our democratic forms of Government. If the functioning mechanism of the State is broken down into smaller democratic units, the State is less likely to develop the power and privilege of a monolith. The ultimate guarantee for democracy is more democracy and

also

more direct democracy. Likewise, the answer to the shortcomings of democracy is/more democracy. However, direct democracy is possible only where the unit is small. That is why Gandhiji had stressed that the village was the ideal unit for democracy. He had emphasised the Gram Sabha to which the Panchayat must be directlyresponsible. It is for this reason that the Gram Panchayat incorporated in the Directive Principles of our Constitution remains the one inevitable component of our Panchayat Raj :system: .

24. The same holds good for the Congress organisation. It is in activising the Village Congress Committees upwards that I see the Party's real revitalisation. I shall advert to this subject a little later.

Fellow delegates, . .

25. This session coincides with unprecedented changes in the world economic relations. By and large, the global economy is facing recessionary trends. International economic relations are undergoing structural changes, following economic compulsions as well as changing geo-political relations. This Session, therefore, provides a historic opportunity to take stock of these developments and to chart the future course of our economic policies for the progress of the Indian people. This is also an excellent opportunity to clear our minds and answer the critics of the Congress logically and effectively.

26. Since the beginning of the era of planned development, the Indian National Congress has been inspired and guided by the vision of Jawaharlal Nehru. His strong sense of history and deep understanding of the distinctiveness of the Indian ethos, led him to reject borrowed doctrinaire approaches and to evolve India's own synthesis from diverse influences, which was inherently just, humane, pragmatic and uniquely Indian.

27.   The use of development planning was an instrument to achieve these ends and to ensure the material well-being of the masses and the dignity of the individual. These became elements of his Socialistic pattern. As we look to the future, the fundamentals of Nehru's vision remain entirely relevant from every standpoint.

28.   This Session is taking place at a time when the Indian economy is facing the gravest crisis since independence. The country was hit by the total mismanagement of its economy during a year and a half   . The situation reached crisis proportions by June 1991. The balance of payments problems became critical and default by us in repayment of foreign debts became imminent. Industrial production was disrupted, exports declined and inflation reached a level of 16.7% in August 1991. A series of corrective measures were announced since July 1991 when the Congress assumed power again. These have succeeded in checking the downward slide and restoring some control over the situation. However, inflation is still high and an uphill task faces the country to return to a satisfactory growth path.

29.   In the past ten months, our Government has initiated far-reaching fiscal and financial reforms. This was done in conformity with our Election Manifesto of 1991 which gives the main features of the reforms. It is remarkable that even when the Congress was in the opposition, the late Shri Rajiv Gandhi anticipated the economic crisis that was coming and incorporated clear and concrete remedial as well as positive measures in the Manifesto. The Government has introduced this reform programme with considerable dynamism. Simultaneously, we have also taken measures to mitigate any hardship likely to be caused in the process. We propose to continue, in fact increase, the thrust of our employment, poverty alleviation and welfare programmes. I must, however, add that these are two parallel and complementary

programmes. Between the two of them all sections of the people are covered, at all levels of the social pyramid, with particular emphasis on the base of the pyramid. As a political party, the dynamic leadership and clear voice of the Congress are needed for the upliftment of the oppressed, even while we carry out reforms in the economy as a whole. This overriding priority needs to be spelt out unequivocally.

30.   There are some who seem to think that in the new context, the basis of Nehru's vision of a socialist India has become untenable. On the other hand, there are some others who allege that we are today giving up his vision, yielding to outside pressures. Let it be clear that we are doing nothing of the kind. We need, therefore, to be clear in our minds where we stand. In a *laissez faire*-society the underlying assumption is that if each person pursues his own happiness the market will ensure the happiness of all. Communism, in the form in which it has failed, assumed that the pursuit of the collective good would automatically result in the happiness of the individual. Clearly, we differ from both these assertions. We have to strike a balance between individual and common good. Indeed there is no contradiction between the two. *It is the virtue of democracy that it permits a variety of such pursuits and their fine-tuning from time to time.*

31.   A country of India's size has to be self-reliant. We have learnt this lesson from our bitter experience both in the industrial and agricultural fields in the first decade of our independence. It is being alleged that we are giving up self-reliance. This is not true. Our concept of self-reliance so far has included an emphasis on building up basic industries within the country and on import substitution. The priority given to basic industries was one of the great contributions of Nehru. It is this which has brought us to the point today where we are able to consider other options with confidence. We believe, however, that the stage has now come when we could review our strategy. Import substitution cannot be an

end in itself. The very level of development we have reached has made us independent of the world economy in some respects, but more dependent on it in others. This is an important aspect of the complexity of modern development. There is hardly any country in the world, howsoever developed, which insists on making everything it needs. Not that it does not possess the capacity to do so, but it finds it more economical, in its circumstances, to buy a number of things from others who make them. Some strategic areas, of course, should be treated as exceptions to this and we have to insist on manufacturing such items within the country. In other cases, the criterion of self-reliance today has to be not whether you can make whatever you need, but whether you can pay for whatever you need. One way of describing self-reliance would be to say that we should be indebted only to the extent we have the capacity to repay. This is also in perfect conformity with the Indian tradition and ethos. Therefore, while we are re-defining self-reliance, we are not abandoning the basic principle.

32.   The other major issue is about foreign capital. At one stage, we gave protection to native capital. This was necessary when we had just emerged from a long period of foreign rule during which everything had been done to cripple our native initiative. We believe that in these four decades of independent development, our indigenous capital has reached a stage where it can stand on its own feet. But the limitations of native capital, both quantitative and technological, pointed to the need of opening up the economy to external replenishment. Besides, the opening up process has its justification on economic grounds.   There is no way for the Indian economy to remain insulated within its confines any longer. It has to integrate itself with the world economy. The two-way traffic of capital, manpower, technology etc. will have to be opened up. We have, therefore, to reorient our previous approach to foreign capital. We are seeking to do so.

33.   However, we have to protect our national interest in the matter of developing science and technology within the country. In the first place, technology does not always flow freely across frontiers. Besides, the recipient country may not find the imported technology suitable or affordable. Therefore, there is every need to protect and encourage science and technology developed within the country.

34.   The other area in which national interest needs to be safeguarded is in the benefit accruing to the people. The mere import of foreign capital has no meaning if it does not bring commensurate benefits to the people. Employment, transfer of technology, fresh opportunities of entrepreneurship etc. should come to the people in a tangible way along with foreign capital.   This is extremely important for any developing country.

35.   The role of the public sector is another issue on which there has been some controversy. The public sector has been a great boon to the country and has largely contributed to industrialisation and the creation of infra-structure. Moreover, it came into existence at a most crucial time in the country's economic history when no one from abroad was ready to help India in the infra-structure area. *The public sector therefore stands as a symbol of the country's self-reliance*. It was the corner-stone of Panditji's vision. It has served the country very well and will no doubt continue to do so.

36.   There are those who complain that we are pulling the public sector down. Let me straight-away clarify that we are doing no such thing. Here also, what we are doing is to re-define the role of the public sector. What exactly is the public sector? It is, in fact, a sector owned by the State, and run with the money belonging to the people. The profits and losses of the public sector, therefore, are the profits and

losses of the people. It has to be admitted that over the decades, the public sector, for various reasons, has not been performing as well as was expected of it. The reasons have been gone into and remedial measures are being adopted in right earnest. In particular, there is no intention of doing away with the public sector, as such. But it is agreed on all hands that the public sector needs to be made more efficient and capable.

37.   At this point it may be pertinent to quote Panditji himself on his vision of the public sector and the dual sector approach in general:

> *"Our national aim is a Welfare State and a socialist economy. Neither of these can be attained without considerable increase in national income and neither is possible without much greater volume of goods and services and full employment. In order to attain this welfare State of a socialist pattern, it is not enough to pass a resolution or even law or to limit our thinking to nationalisation of existing industries. We have to see that there is equitable distribution and that the privileged position of individuals and groups is not favoured.*

> *Everything, therefore, that leads to fuller production and fuller employment is to be encouraged, provided it does not take us away from the ultimate objective of a socialistic pattern of society. If we cannot have fuller production and fuller employment, then there will be neither welfare nor socialism, even though we might nationalise some industries or pass brave laws and decrees. If we aim at mass production, this is only possible if this production is for the masses and the masses have the purchasing power to consume it. We have to introduce a certain dynamism in every sector of our economic and national life in order to achieve this*

*goal. The test must always be the results to be achieved
and not some theoretical formula ...*

*The main purpose of a socialised pattern of
society is to remove the fetters to production and
distribution. If, however, we adopt a policy, in the
name of socialism, which actually maintains some
fetters or encourages them, then we are moving away
from our objective and preventing the growth of full
dynamism. It becomes necessary, therefore, to have a
private sector also and to give it full play within its field,
provided always that it is coordinated with our planned
approach.*

38.   Nehru thus clearly put both sectors in perspective.
Many people admit that the market will not necessarily
respond to basic social needs by itself, particularly if there is
not much profit in the fulfilment of those needs, as often
happens. In such cases, no agency other than the public
sector will meet these needs. Evidently, therefore, there is a
wide field in which the public sector would be required to
play an important role in the interest of the people. This is
particularly so where a pioneering effort involves risks and
precludes the private sector's willing entry, in the first
instance. Such areas will need to be attended to almost
exclusively by the public sector for a long time to come. The
Congress Manifesto of 1991 makes a pointed reference to
this.

39.   We have invested over one lakh crores (1000 billion)
of rupees in the public sector so far. The returns therefrom,
on the whole, have been very meagre, even negative in
several cases. All this is people's money, no one else's. The
present situation is that Government can no longer collect any
more money from the people for further fresh investment in
the public sector. This is an undeniable reality. But if there is
no further investment, the country cannot progress.

Therefore, additional investment has to be procured from outside sources and the private sector has to step in. Our new industrial policies are meant to attract massive investments from within the country and abroad, in the infrastructure and other areas. The prospects are really bright and are becoming brighter by the day, thanks to the Government's new strategy and the inherent advantages available in this country.

The expansion of the public sector, hereafter, has obviously to be more selective, purpose-wise. The emphasis, instead, should be to restore the existing public sector back to health and profitability. In this process of reforming the public sector, we are also taking care to see that hardship to the labour force is avoided. For this, a huge safety net called the National Renewal Fund, has been established. It will assist the workers to the utmost extent...

40. There is, however, one danger which we must recognise and guard against in the "opening up" process. This could lead to wider disparities within the society. To meet this situation, we have to enable the under-privileged sections also to derive the benefit of the new opportunities. This process would naturally need some time to fructify. Until that happens, there has to be a by-pass arrangement whereby benefits reach the lowest rungs of the social pyramid directly from the State. We are doing this.

41. In relation to the agricultural sector, we have to take special measures to see that benefits also flow to it from liberalisation. Agriculture will continue to be the main economic base for a majority of our people for a long time to come. The role of the State in providing the infrastructure and other support to this sector will therefore continue. Increasing agricultural productivity is an important instrument in fighting poverty as well as regional disparities. Therefore, we have to modernise agriculture by the spread of education and introduction of new technologies in the rural economy.

42.   These, then, will be the ingredients of our new socialist policy. They do not represent the withdrawal of the State altogether, but a reconsideration of the areas in which it must be present. At the moment, the State has over-stretched its meagre resources and is seeking to do many things at the same time. In the result, it is unable to do anything adequately. Our weakness lies in the size of our population, but our strength also lies in that population. Admittedly, the competitive advantage of nations today is their human resource.

      Therefore, whichever way we look at this problem, education and health of our people have to get the pride of place in our programmes. It is inconceivable that any private body or individual could run the primary education or primary health care programmes, on a country-wide scale, almost free of cost as they happen to be today. Some private schools and hospitals may be opened, but they will be for those who can pay. For the vast majority of the poor, the State is the sole provider. It is, however, regrettably true that in Plan after Plan, the outlays on education and health, the key areas of human resource development, have received inadequate attention. The main reason for this was the overall priority the planners had to give to the economically more vital sectors such as irrigation, power, fertilisers, etc. These priorities, of course, are also valid. The fact of the matter is that the overall resources at our disposal were themselves inadequate; we had to spread them too wide and too thin. In order, therefore, to shoulder the vital responsibility of human resource development adequately, the State must conserve its resources by withdrawing from various areas where private enterprise can effectively replace it. Besides, the State has certain functions which belong to it by its very nature, such as defence, law and order and governance. Outside these areas, the criterion for State intervention ought to be whether its presence is for the benefit and protection of the poor.

The Scheduled Castes, Scheduled Tribes, Other Backward Classes, minorities and all weaker sections would get greater benefits when the State's responsibility for the creation of large physical assets is transferred to other agencies and its resources available for human resources increase consequently. When this happens, the present social tensions, emanating often from inadequate attention to these sections, will also tend to ease.

43.   Thus, in matters relating to the economy as a whole and in areas of international economic activity and trade, the State's role should taper off gradually. On the other hand, its role should be considerably enhanced in the other area which impinges on the lives of the vast majority of our population. These are the oppressed and the under-privileged for whom life has traditionally been a game of snakes and ladders. Here, the duty of the State is to provide more ladders for the poor to rise and to keep the snakes at least at bay. As Gandhi's party, it is this that should remain our major area of concern, thrust and activity.

44.   The thrust of poverty alleviation programmes will be through Employment Guarantee Schemes and subsidised food distribution to the poor. Proper targetting and linkage of the food programme with employment is necessary, so that food does not become a dole. The Jawahar Rozgar Yojana, Nehru Rozgar Yojana, Indira Awas Yojana, Indira Mahila Yojana, Wasteland Development Programme, National Literacy Mission, Integrated Child Development Services(ICDS) and many other such programmes are in implementation. The Government has just taken up the re-vamped public distribution system, according to which commodities of daily use reach the people in 1700 of the most backward blocks in the country, at subsidised rates. These and several such programmes are, however, crying for active support and attention from people's organisations. If only Congressmen and Congresswomen could get involved in these

programmes, all the people, including other parties and organisations, will follow suit and we shall have a massive national movement of reconstruction. It also becomes necessary to devise programmes which will encourage better asset distribution and the acquisition of assets by those who do not now have them. In the industrial sector one such measure is widening the base of shareholding. In the rural sector this necessarily involves land reforms and distribution of surplus land.

45.   However, whatever we do, we cannot cope with our problems if our population grows at the present rate. Family planning is therefore central to our development. Limiting population and upgrading skills must be our new slogan. I may also add that universal literacy, particularly among women, has turned out to be the largest single factor in the motivation to limit families. The success of the programme has been limited so far, both in area and the extent of the result. It is high time that popular organisations like the Congress take it up in right earnest. Most important, political parties must take this as a national programme, above party interest. I lay emphasis on this aspect, from past experience, which I need not describe further.

Fellow delegates,

46.   The success of these programmes requires their integrated implementation. They should always be responsive to local needs. Local planning has to be the instrument for this and the agency has to be Panchayati Raj. We have introduced a Constitutional Amendment Bill on Panchayati Raj. I find, however, that there is still a lack of clarity, and in some cases even of commitment, for Panchayati Raj because of some weaknesses in it. We have tried to guard against some of them by providing for reservations at every level. We cannot, as political workers, despair of the political process merely because there is some pollution in the process. Such despair should not take us to the other extreme of once again

putting our faith in change through the bureaucracy. We have a fine bureaucracy. We have a number of young persons dedicated to social change. However, social change requires political action. We should not ask the bureaucracy to implement a programme of this kind, without support from political leadership. We must therefore learn to work at every level through the political process offered by the Panchayati Raj institutions, on the one hand, and the functioning of the party at different levels, on the other. There is nothing new in this approach. It is as old as the Mahatma's injunctions, so familiar to everyone. Yet, these very injunctions have been observed in breach for some time. We have to hark back to them today for the Party's sheer survival and in the interests of the people whom we serve.

47.   We often hear complaints of wastage and malpractice in the utilisation of funds granted for developmental programmes at the grassroots level. The Congress Committee at the destination, along with the Panchayat, is best fitted to monitor this aspect. From that point should begin the process of plugging the leakage. We shall soon work out an effective system wherein the Party can play its role in the interest of the people. Not all the Congress workers hanker after posts and positions. What they do want is a useful role. I am confident that in the months to come, the new set-up will fulfil this operation. I have faith in the essential honesty of the average Congressman. Wherever he or she is fully involved, the result will be beneficial to the people, by and large.

48.   I have often felt that we have, for a long time, neglected social reform programmes, in our extreme preoccupation with the political process. This is a serious omission. The social evils that bedevil the Indian society, even in this enlightened era, do not redound to our credit as a nation. Unless Congressmen take up social reform as an integral part of their work, the spate of legislation we have passed over the years will only remain a dead letter. In particular, the atrocities

against women have brought shame to the Nation. I therefore appeal to Congressmen and Congresswomen to return to Mahatma Gandhi's injunction to plunge into a massive country-wide campaign of social reform. There has to be a determined bid to fight against these evils that are eating into the vitals of the society and threaten to destroy it.

49.   I shall now briefly touch upon a few burning problems the country is facing. Details are given in the resolutions you will be considering in a short while. I shall give only brief comments:

The situation in Punjab has entered a steady but crucial stage. Despite terrorist threats held out with aid and abetment from across the border, the people have unequivocally given their verdict for the democratic process. It was a brave and patriotic act, by any standard. I would appeal to all political parties and the people to help in evolving a consensus on the outstanding issues in Punjab. The people want an end to violence. They have a right to a peaceful life and their share of orderly development. We pledge to fulfil their wish. The Congress Government in the State will strive to secure all-round cooperation to this end.

50.   The State of Assam has passed through a most trying decade. The people have once again opted for Congress rule. There are hopeful signs for the return of peace to this troubled State. The State Government will continue to enlist the support of all parties and groups and bring about cessation of violence in the interest of the people.

51.   The State of Jammu and Kashmir has witnessed escalation of violence in the past two years. The dismissal of the elected State Government in 1990 brought about alienation. Here again, the active support from across the border has compounded the situation. By the strenuous and patient efforts made by the Central and State Governments in

·the past ten months, there are hopeful signs of a return to normalcy. It will need time, but the right process has been set in motion. People's involvement in the affairs of the State is of the essence. I am confident that this will become possible sooner than later. In a democratic country, no part should be deprived of a democratic set-up for long. We are directing all our effort to this end, while coping with the problem of violence and secessionist activity.

FOREIGN POLICY

52.   I have dealt with democracy, secularism and socialism. That brings me to Non-alignment. With the far-reaching transformation of the world scene during the past few years, the foreign policies of many countries have tended to undergo changes. The course of these changes is still unclear and the overall situation continues to be fluid. However, the Indian National Congress is convinced that despite these changes, India's foreign policy delineated by Nehru and consolidated by Indiraji and Rajivji is entirely valid and no basic change is called for. For instance, the recent attacks on the concept of Non-alignment and criticism of the Non-aligned Movement, as such, are unwarranted. The role of the Movement will and must change; but the validity of the Movement cannot be called in question.

53.   Though Non-alignment as a movement was launched in 1961, it was a national impulse much earlier. It would be appropriate to regard Non-alignment as an urge for independence in judgement and action, in exercise of the sovereign equality of nations. As a Movement, it would invariably be involved in every problem the world faces. While doing so, it is bound to find itself on different sides of the fence on different issues, since it would insist on judging each issue on merit. Non-alignment is thus the anti-thesis of the Bloc or Group process wherein decisions are taken in

advance, tailored to individual interests. It aims at cutting all strings attached to the processes of free decision-making, thus heralding a new era in relations between nations.

54. The Non-aligned, most of whom are developing countries, have to contend with not only their present problems of balance of payments, inflation etc., but what I consider infinitely more important, their own economic destiny. Blindly aping an affluent economy and way of life, much beyond their means and capabilities, will mean unmitigated disaster to developing countries and erode the essence of their freedom. What needs to be realised is that poverty by itself is nothing contemptible; what is really deplorable is to ignore realities and to barter freedom for what may appear temporary gains. It would be a clear negation of Non-alignment which, essentially, is the preservation of freedom and self-reliance.

55. This self-reliance must consist in trying to find solutions to our/problems primarily according to our own genius. We should therefore persevere in our massive effort to lift ourselves up, as a whole mass and not piecemeal. We must use methods and technology most relevant to our conditions, ranging from the most sophisticated to the most simple. We reject nothing useful for its plainness, we take nothing irrelevant for its dazzle. Many developing countries are now seeing their way to accept this pattern. Some of them have arrived at it by the hard route of disillusionment from inappropriate models.

Fellow delegates,

56. We are discussing Non-alignment at this party, while some others, within and outside the Non-aligned, assert that Non-alignment is irrelevant and therefore dead. This, I submit, is not correct. It ignores the essentials of Non-

alignment, indeed it refuses to' recognise freedom of judgment as an attribute of nations. .

57.   We are living in a time of change, palpable change. Until very recently, the effectiveness of the United Nations Organisation was inhibited by the cold war. We have since witnessed an upsurge of democratic sentiment all over the world. We have been heartened by the desire in. diverse countries that the values of liberty, economic justice and the dignity of man should govern the conduct of world affairs. These are healthy trends indeed.

58.   India's support to the United Nations has been complete and consistent. It has had no fluctuations. Today, we welcome the effective role of the Security Council in matters of peace and security. But lasting peace and security necessarily require comparable levels of human happiness across the globe. It is impossible to think of the United Nations functioning usefully and harmoniously while humankind continues to be riddled with ever-increasing disparities, giving rise to mounting social tensions.

59.   The role of the United Nations must naturally rest on the Charter. However, the interpretation of the Charter as well as the actions by the Security Council must flow from the collective will and not from the views or predilections or a few. A general consensus must always prevail.

60.   As the composition of the General Assembly has trebled since its inception, the size of the Security Council cannot remain constant any longer. Wider representation in the Security Council is a must; if it is to ensure its moral sanction and political effectiveness.

NON-PROLIFERATION OF NUCLEAR WEAPONS

61. We fully share the concerns on the threat posed to international peace and security by the proliferation of nuclear weapons. But the real dimension of international security today is that of the possible loss of control over nuclear arsenals. What we are faced with is no longer the possible acquisition of such weapons by a handful of "threshold" States, but an uncontrolled spread of ready-made nuclear weapons everywhere. This proliferation issue has thus assumed a qualitatively and frighteningly new dimension.

62. What then is the answer to this difficult dilemma? In our view, the only logical route available to us is to pursue a global approach, based on a new international consensus on non-proliferation. To be effective, this global non-proliferation regime must be universal, comprehensive and non-discriminatory. Its goal should be full and complete nuclear disarmament. There should be no reservation on this goal.

ACTION PLAN FOR DISARMAMENT

63. At the third special session of the United Nations devoted to disarmament, held in 1988, our late Prime Minister Rajiv Gandhi put forward a specific Action Plan for Disarmament. The plan contained all the key elements of a new international consensus on nuclear non-proliferation. First, it called for the conclusion of an international convention on the prohibition of the use or threat of use of nuclear weapons. Second, it advocated a comprehensive test-ban treaty. Third, "threshold" States would undertake obligations not to cross the threshold, and this would be linked to corresponding obligations by nuclear-weapon States to eliminate their nuclear arsenals by the year 2010 at the latest

64.   In fact, in view of the recent positive trends, I have suggested that the target date in India's Action Plan for a nuclear weapon-free world should now be advanced to the end of the present century. It would be a hopeful note on which to enter the twenty-first century.

THE MIDDLE WAY

65.   Influenced by the great Buddha, Jawaharlal Nehru tried to mark a middle way for us in all spheres. It was the same in Non-alignment in international relations, or in his concept of mixed economy in a socialist pattern of society. Some seem to think that with the collapse of the Communist system and the world having become uni-polar, there can be no middle way since we have only one way now. It is a moot question whether, in fact, the world is uni-polar or whether there is only one way for the development of societies for all time to come. This forecast is too speculative, and perhaps unrealistic. To interpret Nehru's middle way as being valid only in a bi-polar situation is not to understand our ancient philosophy of the Middle Way. The Middle Way was meant to be a constant reminder that no assertion or its opposite can be the full and complete Truth. It meant that we looked for Truth in the interstices of dogmas. *It means today that we will accept no dogma even if it happens to be the only dogma remaining in the field at a given moment. Our quest for truth will still continue.*

66.   Historic changes have taken place in the world. Some of them have been dramatic in their swiftness, while others will certainly affect the history of humanity. Nevertheless, I would not consider them totally unprecedented. Every great epoch has seen some such event and considered it unprecedented. This apocalyptic appraisal is part of the tradition of the West. We, on the other hand, have always looked at human progression in cycles of rise and fall. We should, therefore, take these changes in a steadier stride.

However, we live in a world dominated by Western ideas. These ideas may not necessarily have deeper insight in all cases, but they have undoubtedly succeeded-- by their arms in the past and their technology in the present. We have to adopt, and adapt to, not only these technologies but all that is wise and humane in the Western tradition. *Yet, while doing so, we have to be securely anchored in our own tradition, which is equally incisive, and much more relevant to our situation.* Likewise, in assessing the Western approach in the present world configuration of forces, we have to adopt an attitude which is assimilative but at the same time detached and critical.

67.   When modern Western civilisation set forth to discover the secrets of Nature, its intention was to conquer it. We, on the other hand, had always looked upon ourselves as a part of Nature and subject to its laws. The new civilisation considered Nature to be at the service of man, purely and simply. And serve it did. Man was thrilled by his mastery of Nature, and exploited it excessively and mercilessly. However, Nature now threatens to commit suicide unless it obtains redress. Modern Western civilisation does not seem to know how to handle this situation. In this confusion, some affluent nations seem to think that putting a lid on further development everywhere would do the trick and save the environment. But in effect, what this will lead to is to keep the under-developed countries perpetually under-developed, while the developed countries more or less retain their present level of development. Obviously, this formula cannot be accepted. Here again, there has to be a prospect of attaining comparable, if not identical, levels of development all over the world, using new and environment- friendly technologies. Those new technologies need to be developed and made available to all needy countries. Any attempt to earn profits at the cost of Environment will be suicidal inasmuch as no one will be left to enjoy the profits, if Nature revolts. Here again,

our late leader Rajiv Gandhi's suggestion for a Planet Protection Fund deserves serious consideration.

68.   The West has also set out on an equally arrogant journey within. We are at the beginning of an era when science will discover man's inner world-- the mind of man-- through computer technology and the genetic code through molecular biology. Once again, they are setting out on this journey, not as one of discovery and understanding, but of conquest. But at the end of this journey, they will again find *us* ahead, because this is one journey we had undertaken long ago. We may not have analysed the structure; but we grasped the essence. They have always pursued the how of things; we have concerned ourselves with the why and wherefore. Human understanding requires both aspects. Now, when Nature is threatening extinction, they are beginning to realise that Truth has many facets some of which *we* had realised earlier. For our part, we can be patient as we have always been. We must meanwhile sustain our self-confidence. We must realise that India is not just another State but a State that constitutes a civilisational centre. And when I mention India in this connection, I do not confine myself merely to the geographical chunk that is called India. It goes far beyond those confines. Here India is not merely a country; it is a concept, it is a vision. In that sense, ours is the experience of an entire civilisation adjusting to and assimilating the experience of another. The greatness of Gandhi and Nehru was that they realised the significance and magnitude of what we had set forth to do. Gandhi represented the very soul of this civilisation-- bare in its externalities but secure in its inner strength. Nehru, like Arjuna, glimpsed the complexity and grandeur of this process. He articulated it for us, the succeeding generations. It is that inner source of strength and grandeur that we must be able to touch in the struggles that we continue to face.

[margin note: civili- sation]

ॐ एकम् सत् विप्रा बहुदा वदन्ति ।

Fellow delegates,

69.　　　　As I conclude this Address, I think of the stupendous task that awaits the millions of Congress Workers in the villages and towns of India. I have the highest respect and affection for the workers who serve silently where they reside, carrying on their usual professions. These part-timers are the back-bone of the Party, who expect no returns, no offices, no posts. These are the messengers of the Congress whose motivation is pure, unselfish and entirely patriotic. Their involvement could be formal where possible, but they could also function with utmost informality and spirit of brotherhood. The face-to-face community makes this possible. It is this huge army of service that has to bestir itself now. It spans three or four generations, beginning with the old freedom fighters who are still happily with us.

This massive effort would have to be shouldered, by and large, by the youth in the Party. This task requires, above everything, idealism and a sense of sacrifice. The Congress has always had the youth in the vanguard of its movement. We of the older generation know full well how *our* leaders had caught us young in those days, while we were students fired with zeal and patriotism. It is the same in every generation. The Youth Congress and the NSUI are the active arm of the Congress. They will always be on call.

Women have contributed as much as men, sometimes more, during the freedom struggle and after. Yet, one cannot help feeling that they have not got their due in our present dispensation. This, I am sure, needs to be remedied at the earliest. We cannot continue to treat half of our population with indifference. This deserves top priority. We shall need their services to the fullest extent in the reorganisation and revitalisation of the Congress and bringing justice to them in all spheres.

70.   For some time now, I have given some thought to the future functioning of the Party organisation. I am happy that each one of you, as also the Congress Committees at all levels, will now be strengthened by legitimacy. You are the recognised bricks and pillars of the Indian National Congress. I compliment you most heartily and look forward to working with you in the great task of building the Party from the village upwards.

I want Village Congress Committees to be formed and activated. Congress offices at different levels should function regularly, attending to people's grievances.   Meetings and rallies should reverberate everywhere. We intend to hold some huge Narora-type camps in the near future, where our ideology and strategy would be discussed and sharpened. It will then spill over to a number of camps at different levels, to create enlightened and well-informed Congressmen and Congresswomen in large numbers.

We have to be particularly careful about funds. Meetings should have voluntary and spontaneous attendance, whether big or small. The Congress Constitution provides for donation by every Active Member, a small percentage of his or her annual income. If systematically implemented, this should keep the Party reasonably well provided. To the extent possible, we shall initiate the method of replacing money with manpower at the elections. If the Party functions regularly, there should be no need to raise clouds of dust from vehicles at election time.

Congress elections have given the Party a shot in the arm. But they have also brought out some weaknesses. While this may have happened because of the elections taking place rather unexpectedly, this should not happen hereafter. Elections should be held regularly according to the Congress Constitution. For this, enrolment of membership should be done continuously. It should be ensured that current office bearers at any levels doe not get any undue advantage in the process. A systematic programme of constructing or acquiring office buildings at least down to the district level, should be undertaken at an early date.

Party literature should be regularly produced and distributed in all languages. A special effort should be made for this.

These are only some of the items that come to my mind. I am sure that the new Congress Working Committee will initiate a dynamic programme of building the Party with many more useful ideas.

This year we will be celebrating the 50th anniversary of the most decisive event in the history of our freedom struggle, the "Quit India Movement". The words of Gandhiji, Sardar Patel and Pandit Nehru in the Shivaji Maidan on 8th August Speak to us today with urgency and excitement. They are not merely echoes from the distant past. The Quit India resolution naturally dealt with Indo-British relations. But even in that moment of great tension and indignation, Gandhi and Nehru did not forget the larger world outside. Reference to a world federation in the Quit India Resolution had great significance. They saw India's freedom as a part of the freedom of all nations. Their breadth of vision shall inform our thinking. Those moments will continue to grip our minds and enoble coming generations. They will inspire posterity to rise to heights of patriotism and sacrifice. I appeal to the people in general and Congressmen in particular to observe the occasion in a fitting manner, the manner in which a grateful nation remembers a noble phase in its history.

71. I have said that despite the effort of the last ten months, the country will demand sacrifices from the people. I am grateful to them for the sympathy and understanding they have shown during this trying period. Economic recovery will take time. The re-establishment of social harmony, after the regrettable experience of communal and caste divides in 1990, will be a gradual process. The Congress has always stood for social justice. This is undeniable. In the past ten months of Congress rule, social tensions have steadily come down. The millions of Congress Workers spread all over the country should now carry the message of love and harmony among the people. I think that all those who belong to the Congress culture should come out of their fragmented nooks. They will have to re-live their role of the freedom struggle days when they had carried the torch of swaraj to every corner of the country. WE WANT 'SURAAJ'. ALONG WITH SWARAJ NOW. THIS SHALL BE THE CALL OF THE TIRUPATI PLENARY. This is the task WE give unto OURSELVES at this sacred spot.

We may say in Hindi - Desh Bachao, Desh Banao. These two go hand in hand. You cannot separate them. Desh Bachao, Desh Banao.

JAI HIND.

Notes and References

INTRODUCTION

3 'it is not because...': Eric Hobsbawm, *On History*, Abacus, London, 1997, p. 303.

6 A vibrant debate: Charles Bettelheim, *India Independent*, Macgibbon & Kee, London, 1968.

6 This view was best articulated: Purushottamdas Thakurdas, ed., *A Brief Memorandum Outlining a Plan of Economic Development for India, 2 vols*, Penguin, London, 1945.

7 All other economic activity: For an excellent analysis of the 'Bombay Plan' see Amal Sanyal, 'The Curious Case of the Bombay Plan', *Contemporary Issues and Ideas in Social Sciences,* June 2010, http://journal.ciiss.net/index.php/ciiss/article/view/78/75, accessed on 27 Mar 2016.

7 'the state has to assume...': Government of India, Industrial Policy Resolution, 1956, http://eaindustry.nic.in/handbk/chap001.pdf, accessed 26 Mar 2016.

7 India chose to 'walk on two legs': For a discussion of the economic determinants of Indian foreign policy see Sanjaya Baru, *Strategic Consequences of India's Economic Performance,* Academic Foundation, New Delhi, 2006.

8 'not to have started a revolution...': Rajni Kothari, 'The Meaning of Jawaharlal Nehru', the *Economic Weekly* (Bombay), Special Number July 1964, p. 1203, http://www.epw.in/system/files/pdf/1964_16/29-30-31/the_meaning_of_jawaharlal_nehru.pdf, accessed 25 Feb 2016.

8 'the Congress system': Rajni Kothari, The Congress 'System' in India, *Asian Survey,* Vol. 4, No. 12. University of California Press, Dec. 1964, pp. 1161-1173.

10 To interpret Nehru's middle way as being valid...: P.V. Narasimha Rao, Presidential Address, Plenary Session of All India Congress Committee, Indian National Congress, Tirupati, 14–16 April 1992. For the full text of PV's presidential address to the AICC, see *Appendix*.

13 In a hard-hitting column published in January 1990: Congressman, 'The Great Suicide', *Mainstream*, Republic Day Special Issue, 27 January 1990, http://www.mainstreamweekly.net/article5438.html, accessed 13 May 2016.

13 PV's biographer, Vinay Sitapati,: Personal correspondence with Vinay Sitapati, April 2016.

15 [Rajiv Gandhi's] reforms: Jagdish Bhagwati, *India in Transition: Freeing the Economy*, Clarendon, 1993, p. 80.

15 The 'credibility' of his initiative: Bhagwati, *India in Transition*, p. 84.

CHAPTER 1: JANUARY: THE POLITICS

20 Chandra decided that: Interview with Naresh Chandra, New Delhi, June 2016.

22 When the Russian supremo, Leonid Brezhnev,: M. K. Rasgotra, *A Life in Diplomacy*, Penguin Viking, 2016, p. 337.

23 M. Narasimham, was advised to tell the Americans: Email interview of Y.V. Reddy, who was Narasimham's executive assistant in the executive director's office at the IMF, May 2016.

23 As US strategic policy guru Henry Kissinger: 'US Policy: A New World Order', *India Today*, 15 Mar 1991.

23 Along with PV and Pranab Mukherjee: M. L. Fotedar, *The Chinar Leaves: A Political Memoir*, HarperCollins, New Delhi, 2015, pp. 140–41.

24–25 Chandra Shekhar's helpful 'pragmatism': Barbara Crossette, 'India in an Uproar Over Refueling of US Aircraft', *New York Times*, 30 January 1991.

25 'spilled some hazardous beans': I. K. Gujral, *Matters of Discretion: An Autobiography*, HayHouse Publishers, New Delhi, 2011, Chapter 46.

26 'was deliberately and consciously...': Chan Wahn Kim, *Economic Liberalisation and India's Foreign Policy*, Kalpaz Publications, Delhi, 2006, p. 180.

31 'Not yet': Interview with Deepak Nayyar, New Delhi, 8 March 2016.

32 'If the Fund cannot extend a lifeline...': Ibid.

32 The government in fact raised the cash margins: For a slightly different account of the events of early 1991 and the role of various personalities, see Shankkar Aiyar, Chapter 1, 'The Bonfire of Vanities' in *Accidental India: A History of the Nation's Passage Through Crisis and Change,* Aleph Book Co., Delhi, 2012.

34 I asked Rajiv Gandhi: R. Venkataraman, *My Presidential Years,* HarperCollins, New Delhi, 1994, p. 438.

35 'On this the President directed me...': Fotedar, *Chinar Leaves,* p. 259.

35 'expressed caution against...': Ibid.

35 Personally I have a high regard...': Venkataraman, *Presidential Years,* p. 475.

35 He was a real Hamlet...': Venkataraman, *Presidential Years,* p. 474.

37 'There is no doubt...': Manmohan Singh, Interview to *India Today,* 31 January 1991, http://indiatoday.intoday.in/story/underlying-health-of-indian-economy-is-not-all-that-bad-manmohan-singh/1/317796.html, accessed 3 July 2016.

38 'Of course the prime minister...': Personal interview with Naresh Chandra, 26 April 2016, New Delhi.

38 'was desperate to save...': Venkataraman, *Presidential Years,* p. 475.

39 'Congress doesn't want...': Sharad Pawar, *On My Terms: From the Grassroots to the Corridors of Power,* Speaking Tiger Publications, New Delhi, 2016, p. 91.

39 he felt 'sorry': Venkataraman, *Presidential Years,* p. 476.

CHAPTER 2: MARCH: THE CRISIS

40 On 1 August 1990, Moody's: The analysis offered here is based on a printed copy of the Moody's and S&P reports on India made available to the author in August 1991 (who was at that time, assistant editor with the Economic Times) by an official of the union finance ministry, Government of India. The author made notes from the reports and returned the documents to the official.

40 'political conditions in India have weakened...': Sanjaya Baru, 'India's Credit Rating: A Study in Uncertainty', *The Economic Times,* 12 August 1991.

41 Moody's noted that: Ibid.

42 Blueprints had been prepared: Montek Singh Ahluwalia, 'The 1991 Reforms: How Home-grown Were They?', *Economic and Political Weekly,* Volume 51, Issue No. 29, 16 July 2016.

43 'Although the Economic Surveys...': Vijay Joshi & I. M. D. Little, *India: Macroeconomics and Political Economy, 1964-1991*, Oxford University Press, Delhi, 1994, p. 64.

45 'The major mistake of macroeconomic policy...': Joshi & Little, *Macroeconomics and Political Economy*, pp. 190-191.

46 'If the present crisis is the greatest...: I. G. Patel, 'New Economic Policies: A Historical Perspective', *Economic and Political Weekly*, Bombay, 4-11 January, 1992, p. 43.

47 In December 1990 Finance Minister Sinha recalls: Yashwant Sinha, *Confessions of a Swadeshi Reformer,* Viking Penguin, New Delhi, 2007, p. 6.

48 As the finance ministry's *Economic Survey*: Ministry of Finance, *Economic Survey 1991-92*, Government of India, New Delhi, p. 6, http://indiabudget.nic. in/es1991-92_A/2%20The%20Payments%20Crisis.pdf, accessed 10 May 2016.

49 'I do not want to go down in history...': Interview with Naresh Chandra, April 2016.

CHAPTER 3: MAY: THE ELECTIONS

52 'she was not interested in active politics': Fotedar, *Chinar Leaves*, p. 263.

52 'A group of individuals, with malicious intent...': Pranab Mukherjee, *The Turbulent Years, 1980-1996*, Rupa Publications, New Delhi, 2016, p. 83.

53 'When I learnt of my ouster from the cabinet...': Ibid., p. 88.

53 'To the dismay of the CWC members...': Ibid, pp. 133-34.

62 Most recent memoirs covering that time: Fotedar, *Chinar Leaves,* pp. 261-269.

62 According to Natwar Singh, Sonia was willing: Natwar Singh, *One Life is Not Enough*, Rupa Publications, New Delhi, 2014 pp. 288–89.

64 'He then asked if, as the largest party...': Mukherjee, *Turbulent Years*, p. 120.

65 'Rajiv had propped up the Chandra Shekhar government...': Pawar, *On My Terms*, p. 92.

65 An *India Today* opinion poll conducted on 20 May: 'How India Voted', *India Today*, 15 July 1991, http://indiatoday.intoday.in/story/exit-poll-rajiv-gandhi-assassination-resulted-in-distinct-swing-in-favour-ofcongressi/1/318502.html, accessed 1 Apr 2016.

65 This 'sympathy wave' in favour of the Congress: David Butler, Ashok Lahiri and Prannoy Roy, *India Decides: Elections 1952-1995*, pp. 38-39; M. L. Ahuja and Sharda Paul, *1989-1991 General Elections in India*, New Delhi, 1992, pp. 107-112.

66 the swing in favour of the Congress after 20 May: Arun Kumar, ed., *The Tenth Round: Story of Indian Elections 1991*, Rupa Publications, Calcutta, 1991, pp. 41-53.

66 While the Congress won 50 of the 196 seats: Ibid, pp. 45-60.

68 He suggests that Sonia had to choose between PV, Pawar and Arjun Singh: Fotedar, *Chinar Leaves,* pp. 262-265.

69 'because he was old and was not in good shape': Pawar, *On My Terms*, p. 101.

69 'An elaborate consensus-building effort was initiated...': Mukherjee, *Turbulent Years,* p. 136.

CHAPTER 4: JUNE: THE GOVERNMENT

76 'Sir, it is slightly worse...': Personal interview with Naresh Chandra, New Delhi, 26 April 2016.

77 Curiously, when Nehru died in 1964: Mohit Sen, *A Traveller and the Road: The Journey of an Indian Communist,* Rupa Publications, New Delhi, 2003, pp. 63, 144 and 239.

77 'professional economists in government...' That is how PV described IG to his grandson, V. Srinivas, an IAS officer of the Rajasthan cadre, when the latter was posted to Washington DC as executive assistant to the Indian executive director on the IMF Board. The grandfather confirmed to his grandson what I had first learnt from Mohit and has since been written about by political journalist Kalyani Shankar in 'The genie in the shadows', *Outlook*, 10 January 2011; also notes from personal interview with V Srinivas in New Delhi on 2 May 2016.

78 As IG recalls, he had to travel around the world: I. G. Patel, *Glimpses of Indian Economic Policy: An Insider's View*, Oxford University Press, New Delhi, 2002, p. 169

78 'a bonfire of industrial licensing': I. G. Patel, 'On Taking India into the Twenty First Century', *Modern Asian Studies,* Vol. 21, No.2, 1986.

79 'Pranab, I cannot tell you why I did not take you into the Cabinet…': Mukherjee, *Turbulent Years*, p. 138.

81 'Dr Manmohan Singh is neither a full-fledged politician nor an officer…': P. V. R. K. Prasad, *PMs, CMs and Beyond: Wheels Behind the Veil*, Emesco Books, Hyderabad, 2012, p. 123.

83 One member of Sonia's coterie: R. D. Pradhan, *My Years with Rajiv and Sonia*, HayHouse India, Delhi, 2014.

85 PV saw through the act: Prasad, *PMs, CMs and Beyond*, p. 199.

86 For all that, PV took to the prime ministership effortlessly: For a first-hand account of the ease with which PV took up leadership responsibilities within days of Rajiv Gandhi's death, read Jairam Ramesh, *To The Brink and Back: India's 1991 Story*, Rupa Publications, New Delhi, 2016.

CHAPTER 5: JULY: THE REFORMS

87 The economy is in a crisis: P. V. Narasimha Rao, Broadcast to Nation, *Selected Speeches, Volume I,* June 1991-92, Publications Division, Ministry of Information and Broadcasting, Government of India, New Delhi, 1993, p. 4.

91 In his account of the gold transaction: C. Rangarajan, '1991's Gold Transaction', *The Indian Express*, 28 March 2016.

91 The journalist Shankkar Aiyar: Aiyar, *Accidental India,* pp. 70-71.

92 The entire exercise was dubbed 'hop, skip and jump': For a first-hand account read C. Rangarajan, 'Hop, Skip, Jump', *The Indian Express*, 10 Nov 2015.

92 The first step was to test the waters: Manmohan Singh interview to Shaji Vikraman, '25 years on, Manmohan Singh has a regret: In crisis, we act. When it's over, back to status quo', *The Indian Express*, 6 July 2016.

94 'My motto is trade, not aid…': The full text of this address is reproduced in Ramesh, *To The Brink and Back*, pp. 67-70.

95-96 'The crisis of the fiscal system… Let the whole world hear it loud and clear…': Manmohan Singh, Budget Speech, Ministry of Finance, Government of India, 24 July 1991, http://indiabudget.nic.in/bspeech/bs199192.pdf, accessed 18 Jun 2016.

97 'All [our] measures were really written about…': Narasimha Rao, *Selected Speeches, Vol I* , pp. 8-9.

98 Varma and Mohan had a policy draft ready: Rakesh Mohan, 'We are certainly more open than US. People still say we are a closed economy and we say sorry sir, sorry sir', *The Indian Express*, 8 Jul 2016.

99 'we might still be able to get the industrial policy reforms through': Ramesh, *To the Brink and Back*, p. 92.

100 Here is something that Rajiv Gandhi: Sudeep Chakravarti and R. Jagannathan, 'Ending the Licence Raj', *India Today*, 15 Aug 1991.

101 'A reformer would have known that...': Gurcharan Das, *India Unbound: From Independence to the Global Information Age*, Penguin Books, New Delhi, 2000, p. 223.

102 There is one danger: Rao, Presidential Address.

104 'Yes, there were times I was guided by Manmohan...': Personal notes from conversations with P. V. Narasimha Rao that I used in writing the paper 'Managing the Politics of the Economy', in S. L. Rao, ed., *Managing the Indian State*, Amexcel Publishers Pvt Ltd, New Delhi, 1999 and All India Management Association, New Delhi, pp. 32-54. A. N. Varma, PV's principal secretary, was a discussant for this paper and agreed with whatever I had said.

105 'Dr Manmohan Singh is allergic to politicians': Prasad, *PMs, CMs and Beyond*, p. 123.

107 while differentiating the 1980s brand of reform: Tributes to Dr Arjun Sengupta, *Rights and Development Bulletin*, Vol. 1, Special Issue, December, 2010.

108 The Dagli committee fired the first salvo: *Report of the Committee on Controls and Subsidies* (Chairman:Vadilal Dagli), Ministry of Finance, Government of India, 1979.

108 In their view economic reforms began: A. Subramanian, K. Kochar, U. Kumar, R. Rajan and J. Tokatlidis, 'India's Pattern of Development: What Happened, What Follows?', in Arvind Subramanian, *India's Turn: Understanding the Economic Transformation*, Oxford University Press, 2008, chapter 2.

109 'To be sure, the growth rate shifted...': Arvind Panagariya, *India: The Emerging Giant*, Oxford University Press, New Delhi, 2008, pp. 16-20.

109 While Subramaniam takes this view: Panagariya, *India*, p. 18; and Dani Rodrik and Arvind Subramaniam, 'From 'Hindu Growth' to Productivity Surge: The Mystery of the Indian Growth Transition', *IMF Staff Papers*, No. 52 (2), 2005.

110 The next year is the first year of the Eighth Plan: Ministry of Finance, *Economic Survey 1989-90*, Government of India, February 1990, p. 140.

111 as an economically dynamic: P.V. Narasimha Rao, 'Global Cooperation and Mega Competition', Speech at World Economic Forum, Davos, Switzerland, 3 Feb 1992 in Rao, *Selected Speeches.*

114 Raju was advised to tie up with an Italian company: That K. V. K. Raju approached Snamprogetti because of the Quattrocchi connection was told to me by a senior government official who was associated with the Andhra Pradesh government's plans to establish a fertilizer plant in the state. A senior Birla official complained to this officer that with Raju establishing links with Quattrocchi the Birlas were worried that they may not secure the license. Their worry was well founded since Raju did manage to get the license.

116 Even as these traditional business groups sought to mobilize support: For more on this read Baru, *Transforming India.*

CHAPTER 6: NOVEMBER: THE PARTY

122 In a series of perceptive comments in the columns of the *Financial Express:* C. P. Bhambri's columns have been collected and published as *Politics in India, 1991-92,* Shipra Publications, New Delhi, 1992. (See Section IV.)

123 'The rank and file, however...': K. K. Katyal, 'From Tirupati to Tirupati', *The Hindu,* 13 April 1992.

123 'Prime Ministership has now become proprietorship': Narasimha Rao, *The Insider,* Penguin India, New Delhi, 1998, p. 675.

123 'He was too shrewd not to be aware of the snakes...': Ibid, p. 708.

124 'break the stranglehold of powerful regional bosses': Ibid, pp. 727-728.

125 'Presiding at Lahore, Jawaharlal declared': Rajmohan Gandhi, *The Good Boatman: A Portrait of Gandhi,* Viking, Penguin Books India, 1995, p. 370

126 'The induction of Rajivji into politics ...': Fotedar, *Chinar Leaves,* pp. 153-154

127 'closest to Mrs Gandhi...': Patel, 'New Economic Policies', p. 177.

128 Not surprisingly, the suggestion was readily accepted: Fotedar, *Chinar Leaves,* p. 140.

128 'Prime Minister Narasimha Rao's genius...': Vinay Sitapati, *Half-Lion: How P. V. Narasimha Rao Transformed India,* Penguin Books, new Delhi, 2016, p. 304

131 The rise of regional parties and regional business: See Sanjaya Baru, 'Economic Policy and the Development of Capitalism in India: The Role of Regional Capitalists and Political Parties', in Francine Frankel, et al, eds.

Transforming India: Social and Political Dynamics of Democracy, Oxford University Press, Oxford, 2000.

132 Manmohan Singh became the first nominated: 'President appoints Manmohan Prime Minister', *The Hindu*, 20 May 2004. The Hindu lead story stated: 'Earlier, Dr. Singh was "nominated" the 'Leader of the Congress Party in Parliament to form the government,' after Ms Gandhi stepped down as the leader and was instead elected CPP chairperson. It was in her new capacity as CPP chairperson that she 'nominated' Dr Singh to head the government.'

CHAPTER 7: DECEMBER: THE WORLD

137 'No doubt Narasimha Rao's initial observation...': Nikhil Chakravartty, 'Refashioning Indo-Soviet Relations', *Mainstream*, 31 August 1991. Reproduced in *Mainstream*, 27 August 2011, http://www.mainstreamweekly.net/article2961. html, accessed on 1 June 2011.

137 'I am quite sure that a large country like the Soviet Union...': Rao, *Selected Speeches, Volume I*.

140 She stopped short of expressing her 'understanding': J. N. Dixit, *India's Foreign Policy 1947-2003*, Picus Books, New Delhi, 1998, p. 139.

141 But despite tentative Indian efforts there was no qualitative change: Ibid, p. 151.

142 The budget will mark a major departure...': Yashwant Sinha, 'Budget 1991—Options', *The Economic Times*, New Delhi, 1 July 1991.

143–144 'In my 31 years of service I never once...': Quoted in Chan Wahn Kim, *Economic Liberalisation and India's Foreign Policy*, Kalpaz Publications, Delhi, 2006, p. 36.

144 'The work is cut out for our missions abroad...': Kim, *Economic Liberalisation*, pp. 177-78.

146 European geopolitical analysts have only recently begun: Sanjaya Baru, 'Understanding Geo-economics and Strategy', *Survival: Global Politics and Strategy*, Volume 54, Issue 3, June-July 2012, International Institute for Strategic Studies, pp.47-58. Also, Hans Kundnani, 'Germany as a Geo-economic Power', http://www.ecfr.eu/article/commentary_germany_as_a_geoeconomic_power, accessed 8 June 2016.

147 In PV's time, when US still enjoyed overwhelming military power:

Samuel Huntington, 'Why International Primacy Matters', *International Security*, Volume 18, Issue 4, 1993.

148 'Talking about foreign policies, the House must remember...': For an elaboration of this argument see Baru, *Strategic Consequences*.

149 Narasimha Rao's stewardship: Dixit, *India's Foreign Policy*, p. 221

CHAPTER 8: THE MIDDLE WAY

152 'activist intelligentsia, claiming a right of direction...': Robert Skidelsky, *John Maynard Keynes: The Economist as Saviour, 1920-1937*, Macmillan, London, 1992, p. 406.

153 the 'Indira generation' among economic policymakers: There is now considerable literature on the issue of dating the turnaround in the Indian economy. See for example, Subramanian et al, 'India's Pattern of Development', in *India's Turn* and Panagariya, *India*.

153 They would differentiate their own 1980s brand of reform: Tributes to Dr Arjun Sengupta, Rights and Development Bulletin, Vol. 1, Special Issue, December, 2010, http://www.cdhr.org.in/wp-content/uploads/2015/02/Arjun-Sengupta-Remembrance-Issue-CDHR-Bulletin.pdf, accessed 12 Aug 2016.

153 Was the acceleration of growth: See, for example, Dani Rodrik and Arvind Subramanian, 'From "Hindu Growth" to Productivity Surge: The Mystery of the Indian Growth Transition, *IMF Staff Papers* Vol. 52, Number 2, 2005, https://www.imf.org/External/Pubs/FT/staffp/2005/02/pdf/rodrik1.pdf, accessed 10 Jul 2016.

155 In the past, self-reliance had been defined: This is an idea that has been elaborated at length in Baru, *Strategic Consequences*.

156 'a clever calf sucking two cows': Ibid, Chapter 2.

156 PV's 'middle way' is not to be confused with a 'middle path': Many make the mistake of thinking PV merely sought to strike a balance, pursuing a 'middle path' between the state and market.

156 'seeking truth from facts': Originally a phrase used by Mao Zedong to defend his decision to liberate the Chinese communists from Stalinist orthodoxy in the interpretation of Marxism-Leninism, the guidance 'seek truth from facts' was used by Mao's successor Deng Xiaoping to challenge Maoist orthodoxy within the Chinese communist party. Narasimha Rao's interpretation of the middle way comes close to this dictum of basing political action on a realistic assessment of social, political and economic realities.

157 I tried to explain all these things to my colleagues: P. V. Narasimha Rao, *Ayodhya: 6 December 1992*, Penguin Viking, New Delhi, 2006, p. 188. For an account of what transpired on that fateful day, read Sitapathi, *Half Lion*. Sitapati believes that 'two demolitions' had been planned that winter—the demolition of the disputed structure in Ayodhya and the demolition of PV's prime ministership.

159 Students of the process of modernization: Hobsbawm, *On History*, p. 15.

Index